Loose Ends

Copyright 2008 - Les Combs
Published by Lulu.com

First edition 2008

Printed in the United States of America

ISBN: 978-1-4357-0963-8

LOOSE ENDS

Short Stories and Poems

By Les Combs

In Appreciation

Special thanks to Christie Smith, The Quotable Quill, www.quotablequill.com, for her layout and design skills and for her guidance through publication, to Cynthia Borris author of *No More Bobs* for her editing and to the members of Creative Energy Unlimited and Conway Creative Writers for their help and encouragement.

Table of Contents

1. Harry B. 1
2. Job's Curse 7
3. So Big 11
4. And The Angels Sing 13
5. Do Us Part 20
6. Amana 22
7. That Bobby Earl 26
8. Fore 32
9. Here's to EAP 36
10. Tumbleweed 37
11. Herd Animals 82
12. Forbidden Fruit 84
13. Dance 90
14. Hazel 93
15. Fire in the Hole 118
16. My Brother's Keeper 120
17. Scars 125
18. Call Me Jerry 134
19. C in C's Woman 139
20. The Sunny Gardens Affair 151
21. The Favorite 160
22. Winter Weary 166
23. Let it Be, Let it Be 166
24. Groceries 168

25. The Center 174
26. Old Friends and Acquaintances....................178
27. Twenty-five Cent Peaches............................181
28. That Woman 186
29. Prunus Persica 192
30. Oh Bury Me...197
31. The Bus Stops Here.......................................201
32. The Ceremony 206
33. The Piano...212
34. Uncle Dob...214

Harry B.

I shifted from one foot to the other in front of my editor's desk while he barked into the phone. He'd summoned me from O'Grady's. I'd no more than walked into that dimly lit refuge, intent on having one quick belt, when the phone at the end of the bar rang. O'Grady answered, looked at me and mouthed, "Are you here?" I nodded, and he said into the phone, "Just walked in."

I don't know how Poston did it, but he always seemed to know my location. I'd considered giving myself pat-down searches for a homing device. A crusty old bird, he made a career of terrorizing his reporters. He slammed the phone in its cradle and focused on me, shaggy brows converging over his meaty nose.

"Billups, I've had word about a devil-worshipping cult that's raising hell over in Arkansas. I think you're the man for the job." I read malice in that last sentence in spite of his twisted smile. "Drive your own car, make damned sure you record your mileage, and hang onto your receipts." He gave me the fish-eye, daring me to protest. "You can leave in the morning, save one night's motel bill." He began pawing through papers on his desk, and I realized I'd been dismissed.

"Uh, Boss, I don't suppose you know what part of Arkansas I'm headed for?" Without looking up he pushed a paper through the desk clutter toward me. I gave him a mock salute and made for the door.

The note read, "See Fason DeWitt in Harmony, AR." It was mid-afternoon the next day, and I pushed my eight-year-old Lumina down I-40 faster than prudence would dictate. I'd made a late start due to my commiserating with O'Grady far into the previous evening. I munched an apple from the bag of mixed fruit I'd purchased. My stomach, in its delicate condition, grumbled.

A confirming glance at the open road atlas on the seat next to me, and I took the Clarksville exit. On a secondary road I located the town of Harmony, a blue dot on the map, not many miles into the hills. I stopped at DeWitt Grocery & Gas. Inside I found Fason.

Cadaverous was the only adjective I could come up with to describe the man. Thin and leathery, his face had the look of taxidermy failure. One pale gray eye sighted at thirty degrees to its brown counterpart. He sat with one hip on the checkout counter, a feather duster sticking out of a rear pocket, a can of Mountain Dew clutched in his hand. "Good afternoon," I greeted him.

He nodded and took a swig from the green can. "Sir, my name is Harry Billups." I offered my hand, which he ignored. "I'm with The Mid-South Times-Mirror."

"You selling subscriptions?" he croaked. His voice had the quality of a spring night in the wetlands.

"No sir, I'm a reporter, and I understand you can tell me something about a devil cult operating in this area." His eyes did something funny. I'd swear that the last time I noticed, the brown one was on the left and

Loose Ends

the gray one on the right. No matter.

He stood and faced me or, rather, looked down on me. The man was six-eight if he was an inch. "Can't tell you nothing about that," he said, his mounted-trophy face inches above mine. "Outsiders aren't welcome. It could be hazardous to your health"

Not easily deterred, I pushed ahead. "Sir, I drove all morning to get here. This assignment is important to me." His eyes may have changed back, I couldn't be sure. The brown one seemed to bore into me.

"I can take you to a meeting tonight so you can see for yourself, but don't say I didn't warn you." I agreed to meet him right here "at the crack of dark," as he put it.

There being no business district in Harmony, I returned to Clarksville to while away the remaining hours of daylight in a tavern I'd be ashamed to die in. But the beer was cold and the bartender not unfriendly.

With only a smudge of gray on the western horizon, I parked in front of DeWitt Grocery & Gas. No more than five minutes passed until a caravan of assorted vehicles stopped on the highway. A pickup truck rolled up beside the Lumina. A figure clad in a white sheet and a Richard Nixon rubber mask motioned for me to follow. God, I loved that nose.

Several miles upcountry on the secondary road we branched onto a tertiary road. A mile or so farther, the parade turned onto a quaternary road, a dirt track, and I followed for a quarter-mile to an abandoned barn.

More ghostly figures, twenty or so, exited cars and trucks and milled about in my headlights. All wore facemasks; several Ronald Reagans, two Jimmy Carters, a couple of David Lettermans, a few Henry Kissingers and one Hillary Clinton. Either they had attended a Halloween grab-bag sale or the cult had an eclectic pantheon of deities. I wished I'd brought my Groucho getup. All sported the linen-closet motif. Wal-Mart must have had one helluva white sale. My car door opened, and Hillary beckoned me to follow.

The Springmaid brigade closed around us, and we all entered the board-and-batten building. Gas lanterns, hanging from support posts, lit the cavernous interior. The bed-sheets formed a circle with me standing ill at ease in the center. I had my notepad and ballpoint at the ready, as if to record impending events, but my hands shook.

A king-size percale broke through the outer ranks, a swaying censer held out front. It had to be DeWitt behind the Nixon mask. Bilious green smoke rolled from the metal container and settled earthward.

"O Burning Focus! I have come into Thee; I have cast about me the robe of the waters; I have girt myself with the girdle of knowledge," he intoned in DeWitt's amphibian voice. This was pretty flowery language for Milhaus. I hoped it wouldn't be a long service.

He held the pot over my head while fog the color of pond scum descended over my body. "From the skull of his head hang down a thousand thousand myriads of hair. All are in order." I couldn't guess what this guy's reading habits were, but they gave me the creeps.

While I reached up to scratch an itchy spot on my head, the lights blinked out as one. In the next minute, automobile engines coughed and started. I could hear them leave amid the sound of grinding gears and bad mufflers. I was alone.

I groped my way to the door and saw my car, solitary in the moonlight. Geez, my head itched. I retraced the rough roads, roared through Harmony well above

Loose Ends

the posted limit and pulled into a motel at Clarksville. The Pakistani night clerk darted furtive glances at me while I registered and offered my credit card.

In room 106 I opened my bag and retrieved my shaving kit. I felt grungy, in need of a shower and shave. I walked into the bathroom and stopped short, almost turned and ran. I'd seen dogs do that; come tearing up to something that turned out to be scary, then flip ass-over-tea-kettle to get away.

An unfamiliar image stared back from the mirror. Reddish-gold hair, thick and four inches long, tufted from its head. The growth started above the eyebrows and extended inside the shirt collar, covered the ears. I could be mistaken for a rain-forest tree-dweller.

I tore open my shirt and choked back a scream. A deep-pile, brassy-red growth carpeted my chest. The thing in the mirror glared at me, Harry Billups transformed into a Clint Eastwood co-star.

A hot shower and shampoo did little but expose the extent of my pilose condition. Like a creeping fungal infection, the hair spread southward. Naked, I leaned toward the mirror for a closer look and shuddered.

Divorced and alone, semi-alcoholic, facing a mid-life crisis, I was sunk in despair. And that was yesterday, before the hair thing.

Restless, I swung with one hand from the swag lamp, until it tore loose from the ceiling. In my car I found a leftover banana. I scampered up a huge oak tree next to the parking lot, finding solace among its lofty branches.

It's funny how a banana and a high perch can change one's perspective. A few minutes ago, despondent, I reflected on suicide. Now I felt purged, re-born. I leaped from branch to branch in an expression of joy. In my best Tarzan imitation I thumped my chest and shrieked with gladness. Motel room lights popped on. How delightful, how utterly marvelous to be alive, filled with animal vitality.

I could hardly wait to see the look on old Poston's face when I reported back tomorrow. Banana in hand, I'd request Workman's Comp.

Job's Curse

Me and the god of Abraham, Isaac and Jacob had a disagreement, a difference of opinion. I don't know how big a problem it was for Him, but it was a sure-enough trial for me.

Everybody knows God is a Democrat. I learned that early in life. Entire generations of my family having been rabidly yellow dog in their thinking. Sometime during the last presidential campaign I changed my allegiance and decided to vote for the other party. This act of secession was not widely known. In fact, it was a secret between me and, as it turned out, God.

Knowledge of His interest in the matter came in dramatic revelation the Sunday morning before election day. It happened on the road to Damascus. That's Damascus, AR 72039. My folks live out that way, and I often drive up for Sunday dinner.

I'd just passed Greenbrier when a voice boomed out, "BOY, WHO YOU GOING TO VOTE FOR?" James Earl Jones in Surround-Sound.

There's not a lot of room in the cab of a pickup, but I looked all around, made sure the radio wasn't on, even craned my neck to check the empty bed through the back glass.

"LET'S HEAR THE TRUTH NOW, BOY. WHO IS IT?"

I'm not one to be pushed around by just anybody, and my temper got the best of me. "I don't believe that's anybody's damn business but my own."

"YOU BETTER WATCH THAT MOUTH, BOY."

Man, I never knew you could get that kind of echo in a truck cab.

"I'M GOING TO SEE TO IT THAT YOU GET YOUR MIND RIGHT."

It wasn't a second later that I felt some discomfort in the vicinity of my wallet. By the time I got to my folks' house I was shifting position on the seat, looking for relief.

"That's ugly," Mama said. I lay facedown across the bed, pants around my knees, while she applied a poultice to the flaring red boil on my right cheek. "How long have you had that?"

"Not long, Mama. Do you think that stuff will cure it?" She'd whipped-up a paste of sulfur and mineral spirits, smeared it on a sanitary napkin and Scotch-taped it across the tender area.

"Hard to say, Son. It's in God's hands now." Well that was comforting to know. I ate dinner standing up.

Driving home was possible only because of Mama's pink satin pillow borrowed off the couch. The radio offered no solace. Every station carried church services. Preachers hollered about sin and punishment, choirs sang of repentance and forgiveness. In a highly agitated state I clicked the radio off. With one ear cocked I half hoped for a bargaining session from on high but heard no thundering voices. The lonesome sound of tires on the pavement brought no relief from my pain.

Monday morning, after a sleepless night, I held a

hand mirror to view my bottom reflected in the bath-room full-length glass. A rosy Mount Erebus greeted me, angry and throbbing. Purple rivers of inflamma-tion extended from a base the size of an Oreo cookie.

"HA-HA-HA. NOW THAT'S UGLY." He was back, loud as before and showing a mean streak.

My neighbor in the next apartment pounded on the wall. "Turn it down!" The guy was a crank who frequently complained about the volume on my hi-fi. Anybody who doesn't appreciate Bob Wills music must be sick.

God wasn't done with me.

"CHANGE YOUR MIND YET, BOY?"

Always cool, I maintained my bent-over position. If He wanted a good look, let Him get an eyeful.

More wall pounding. "I'm trying to sleep in here. Turn it down, for God's sake!" If this went on much longer I'd be evicted, thrown out in the parking lot with an erupting boil on my bottom.

"KNOCK IT OFF IN HERE, BUDDY, OR YOU'RE GOING TO HAVE REAL TROUBLE."

This time the booming voice came from the next-door apartment, the sound muffled a bit by the walls. The neighbor's complaints abruptly ended. Not another peep to this very day.

"TOMORROW'S ELECTION DAY, BOY. I KNOW YOU'LL DO THE RIGHT THING."

He left me staring into the mirror and not liking what I saw. I began to wonder if the road to indepen-dent thought might have a few too many bumps.

I was among the first at the polls Tuesday morning. The minute I brought the lever down on a straight-ticket Democratic vote, I felt whole again. The pain vanished as suddenly as it had come. I walked to my truck with jaunty step.

"NOW THAT WASN'T SO HARD, WAS IT, BOY?"

I suppressed a smart-assed retort and got in my truck. Don't ever underestimate the power of a political activist.

So Big

Every year about the time winter has me numb
I wait beside the mailbox for the carrier to come.

Communication from the gods of harvest, I remember,
Seed catalogs, hope eternal, are posted in December.

Full-color illustrations make the heart beat ever faster;
Early Girl, Better Boy, Celebrity, Beefmaster.

Tomatoes every size and shape, how sweet the taste conjured
By pictures on those pages of vines and fruit matured.

A new variety, hybrid, rates a full-page color spread,
Bertha Busby's Bumptious Behemoth Beefsteak Red.

"Huge!" the caption reads in understated prose.
"One will feed a family!" Is it true? Heaven knows.

The name itself confounds reasoned understanding.
Visions rise from the text, reaching out, demanding.

I must have this tomato by all that's right and good.
Envy green will consume the entire neighborhood.

The seeds arrive ere March wind commences with its blowing.
Tiny sprouts soon beneath violet light are growing.

Each plant in turn wilts and dies, to my consternation,
Save one that struggles all alone with grim determination.

It clings to life, somehow survives, and on the first of May
Is planted in the garden to enjoy the light of day.

It quickens even as I watch, with promise to endure.
Hastily I enrich it with composted steer manure.

Upward, ever upward, the vine extends its reach
Until by June it stands above fruit trees, plum and peach.

It blooms and bears and still it grows, towering overhead.
Neighbors come to gawk at it. Jealous tears are shed.

The fruit are of dimension never seen before by men.
Big ones guessed at thirty pounds, the smaller ones at ten.

Expectations are fulfilled in no uncertain terms,
But you should see the size of the horned tomato worms.

They feed upon the plant, appear from unknown sources.
Droppings mound upon the ground much like
Clydesdale horses'.

They chew away remorselessly, starting at the crown.
Leaves and fruit disappear, the stalk turns ugly brown.

I weep among the carnage and give it up for dead,
Bertha Busby's Bumptious Behemoth Beefsteak Red.

And The Angels Sing

A week before Christmas the Tibbses house burned. I'd rode out that morning to feed the cows like I did every winter morning. There're four feed barns on the ranch. Sikes he takes care of two, and I handle the others.

After I finished the first, I rode Chester up the last hill, the one that overlooked the second barn. Chester was a blue-roan gelding with an easy gait, about as nice an animal to get along with as you'd ever run across. I despise being pounded by the saddle on these six-mile rides the way some other horses will do you.

I saw smoke pouring out of their attic as soon as I topped the rise. Farley Tibbs and his wife, Helen, own a little place along the south side of the Rocking H where I work. They have two sections, 1280 acres, not hardly enough to run ninety mama cows. Like I was saying, their house is close to our south fence.

I kicked Chester into a gallop, and by the time I reached the barbed-wire gate, flames spouted up through the roof. Sparks flew high overhead and drifted downwind. If the grass hadn't been wet from last night's rain the whole county would have been fighting a range fire.

Farley and Helen stood huddled together in the

yard like a pair of homeless dogs. There wasn't anything could be done to save the house. Helen she was bad pregnant and looked like she could lay down and deliver any time. She's a right pretty woman, tired looking but with a delicate face like one of those cameo pins. She had tears on her cheeks.

I rode up beside them, tipped my hat to Helen and told them, "Howdy." There's not much you can say to folks at a time like that.

Farley, he's a string-bean kind of guy. Nearly works himself to death ranching. "Well, it looks like we can't do nothin' here until the fire cools out." It sounded like he was already thinking about rebuilding.

They sure looked lonesome standing in their yard watching the flames die down. I said, "Farley, why don't you take Helen over to the bunkhouse? There's just four of us there now, plenty of room." I knew they didn't have any folks around close, and I knew they couldn't afford a motel in town. They looked at each other and nodded.

Farley raised his face to me, hands in his hip pockets. "That's right neighborly of you. Maybe just for tonight."

They drove through the gate in Farley's rattle-bang truck. I closed the gap after them and went to finish my feeding.

When I got back to the ranch the Tibbses were settled in. The boys had partitioned-off the far end of the bunkhouse with hung blankets for privacy. Everybody was kind of walking on eggshells, pretending they always talked mild language in near whispers. Helen was the first woman guest we'd had in the bunkhouse, if you didn't count those two whores from Alder Creek. Sikes and Ketchup brought the pair in one Saturday night.

Fourth of July weekend, I believe it was.

Ketchup was in the kitchen fixing dinner, it being nearly noon. His real name was Irby Ketchum, but the boys gave him the name of Ketchup, which he didn't complain about much. He's our cook and tends to the garden and the chickens and milks the cow.

Me and Sikes and Alejendro sat at the table, as far away from the hanging blankets as we could get. We couldn't seem to get a conversation started, what with the whispers and all. Sikes, he's about half deaf, and he'd roar, "What's that?" every little bit. Me and Alejendro got to laughing about that, and then we just forgot about trying to talk.

We convinced Farley to stay on past that first night so Helen could rest. They didn't have no place to go anyway. Alejendro took time off from working the ranch horses and mending bridle reins and such, his usual job. He helped Farley do his feeding and what little work needed doing over there this time of year.

It commenced to snow Christmas Eve morning. Chester's dark tracks stretched behind us as far as I could see when I went to feed. His nostrils blew smoke, and he acted frisky as a colt the whole ride.

I looked forward to this Christmas Eve. In past years it had been a lonesome time for all of us, four single guys with no close families. We'd sit apart and barely speak. First one and then another would get up and go stare out the window, thinking about lost loves, lost families and lost opportunities.

This year there was a woman in the house. We cut us a small cedar tree that Helen and all of us decorated. We popped corn and strung it on thread. Ketchup came up with some shiny cookie-cutters shaped like hearts and flowers and the like. Lord knows what he was doing with them, he never had baked any cookies. Helen cut an angel out of a magazine to stick on top of the tree. It looked right nice when we finished.

When I walked into the bunkhouse after feeding, I could tell right off that something was up. Sikes and Alejendro looked glum as calves that had just been weaned and branded. Ketchup stuck his head out of the kitchen door every little bit, eyed the blanket curtains and retreated to his pots and pans. "What's going on?" I asked.

Alejendro said, "She's started labor."

"You mean Helen?"

"I don't mean Ketchup," he snorted. "She started about an hour ago."

Farley parted the curtains and hurried to us. He had all the composure of a stampede on a dark night. "Do any of you know anything about deliverin' babies?" I'd never seen anybody fall apart like Farley had. He had jangling nerves if I'd ever seen any. His hands twitched, and he looked like he might pop his neck the way he kept twisting his head to look over his shoulder. Delivering babies? We all shrunk back a step, mumbling idiotic disclaimers. "What are we going to do?" Farley whined, desperate. "I need… she needs help."

Ketchup had come out of the kitchen by now. He suggested, "Maybe we could go get D'arcy and Tillie."

"Aw, Ketchup, they're whores." Sikes cut a quick look at the curtains, and then lowered his voice. In an urgent whisper he said, "You can't bring two whores in here with Miss Helen." The boys had taken a liking to Farley's wife and felt protective of her.

The nearest doctor was sixty miles away. No telling

how bad the snow would be before it quit. Ketchup's idea seemed like our best hope. I turned to Sikes. "Go round 'em up," I told him. "Don't take no for an answer, and get them two ladies back here as quick as you can." Sikes didn't argue. He grabbed his coat and hat and took off like a scalded dog. Farley disappeared back through the curtains.

The noise level from behind the blankets built up, moans coming closer together all the time. Whenever Helen'd holler we exchanged scared looks, and Ketchup's face went pale. He had a dishtowel in his hands and wrung it until he near about tore it in two. It wasn't hardly an hour before Sikes was back with the ladies.

Tillie, she was a chunky woman, dark-haired and calm as a milk cow. D'Arcy was flighty and could have used a few more pounds on her lanky frame. When they came in, Tillie went straight through the curtain, business-like. D'Arcy fussed and fumed. "You owe me, Sikes." She was in his face and not very happy. "I had to give that trucker his money back after you handed him his pants and told him to hit the road."

Sikes shrugged it off, pulled out his wallet and handed her a five-dollar bill. "Here, take it and be quiet. Go help Tillie and try to make yourself useful."

D'Arcy grabbed the five. "Five dollars? Five lousy dollars? You think I'm just a cheap whore you can buy for five dollars? Cheapskate." She pouted like she was highly insulted. Sikes handed her another five. "That's more like it," she told him and headed for the curtains.

After awhile we heard Tillie order Farley out. She followed him through the curtains and told Ketchup to bring her hot water, towels, white thread and who knows what all. Farley looked like death warmed over and moped around, useless as tits on a boar hog.

Then we heard a cry. We all looked at each other like it was the last thing we ever expected to hear. Ketchup started to bawl. His shoulders shook and tears streaked his craggy face. I never knew a man could be that emotional. It didn't make it any easier for the rest of us, neither. Alejendro turned away and blew his nose into a red bandana, and Sikes rubbed at his eyes. Farley disappeared through the curtains again.

After awhile, Farley came out carrying a clean towel bundled in his arms. He looked like a man who'd died and gone to heaven. His face had color again and he wore a watermelon smile. "Folks, this here's my daughter," he said, soft but proud like.

We all gathered up close, and Alejendro asked him, "What are you going to name her?"

Farley stared at him, blank as a slate, for a second. "I guess I need to ask Helen about that." He pulled the towel back so we could take a look. She was a tiny thing, almost lost in the towel. She had dark hair, and you could tell she would have Helen's pretty features. But there was a birthmark on her right cheek, grape-juice colored and about the size of a silver dollar. It wasn't round like a dollar but irregular shaped.

Ketchup peered in, straightened up and said, "It looks like an angel." Then he started bawling again. I swear nobody needs to see a grown man blubbering. It's not a natural sight. I took a closer look at the mark. It didn't look anything like an angel to me, more like a map of Asia. But everybody else agreed with Ketchup, so an angel it was. Helen must have thought so too, because she announced that the baby's name was Angela.

Later that evening, after things had settled down,

we all sat around the stove drinking coffee. It must have been after midnight. Farley had taken the blankets down so Helen could see the Christmas tree. Tillie began to sing *Silent Night*. We all joined in, soft-like because there didn't seem to be any canaries among us. Ketchup broke-down again, but we made it through *Jingle Bells* and ended up with *Hark the Herald Angels Sing*.

Helen told us afterward it was the nicest thing she ever heard.

By mid-April The Tibbses house was rebuilt. Farley worked every daylight hour that weather permitted. The rest of us helped when we could. I rode out that way to feed one day. Spring was in the air, and Chester was feeling coltish. We topped the ridge looking down on the Tibbses new home. Smoke curled from a stone chimney. I opened the gate and rode over to their back porch.

Farley opened the door, Helen standing behind him holding Angela in her arms. "Got time for a cup of coffee?" he asked.

"You bet," I answered.

Do Us Part

"What the devil is that?"

"Adam! Watch your mouth. You need to show more respect. That happens to be a woman."

"Woman?"

"A female. You are a male, she is female."

"Oh. Where did she come from?"

"She came from you, Adam, from one of your ribs."

"No kidding. Why is she so… funny looking? What are those…?"

"Never mind about that now, Adam. Stop pointing and making comments and just take her with you."

"Well, what is it she does?"

"She's your helpmate. She will follow you all the days of your life, care for you, bear your children."

"Children?"

"Wake up and smell the coffee, man! You do want children, don't you?"

"Yeah… I reckon."

"Of course you do. Now get out there and be fruit-ful—populate the world. By the way, her name is Eve."

"Adam?"

"What?"

"Adam, do you not think I am beautiful?"

"What on earth are you talking about?"

"Am I not pleasant to look upon?"

"Sure. You know… I really wanted a dog, a hunting companion, someone to talk to and help keep me warm of a night."

"Oh, Adam, I can do all that for you."

"You hunt?"

"No, silly. Adam, look at me. Take a really good look and tell me what you see."

"Well… your hair is longer than mine."

"I'm not talking about that. Wouldn't you like to kiss me?"

"What do you mean?"

Put your arms around me—like this. Now, press your lips against mine. Like this."

"Oh! Oh!"

"What is it, Adam?"

"I thought I heard a dog bark. Don't run off, I'll be right back."

Amana from Heaven

I'm ashamed to tell how I died. I mean it was so dumb it was embarrassing. I drove to my apartment building this morning to get some papers I needed and had forgotten. Preoccupied, I dashed from my car without bothering to look around... or up.

I failed to notice a refrigerator being hoisted to a third-floor balcony. There's no elevator in the building, and I guess this route looked easier to the deliverymen than three flights of stairs.

When a distraught voice yelled, "Look out!" I reacted in time to see the bottom of an almond frost-free Amana blocking out more sky with each passing millisecond. Can you believe it? Done in by a bunch of Iowans.

I know. You think this story is going to be like that old joke. The one where three guys were in the Pearly Gates reception room. St. Peter called the first one over and said, "What happened to you?" The guy said, "I was on the sidewalk outside this apartment building, and a refrigerator fell on me." St. Peter directed him to another office and called the second guy over. "What's your story?" The second guy said, "My wife has been cheating on me, and I came home early to try to catch her in the act. I rushed upstairs, threw open the door and there was my wife in a negligee. I couldn't find anyone else in the apartment. It made me so angry I picked up the refrigerator and threw it out the window. All the stress and exertion caused a heart attack." St. Peter nodded, sent him on his way and called the third guy. "Let's hear it," he said. "What's your story?" The third guy said, "I was hiding in this refrigerator..."

My story may begin like the joke, but there the similarity ends. In the first place there is no Pearly Gates reception room. It's more like an army induction center, only bigger. You know how many people process through there every day? Millions. It's a growth industry. Lot's of organization is needed for an operation of that scale. They run a very tight ship.

I happened to be in a stream of people entering, twelve-abreast, through Gate IV. Aesthetic-looking cadre in mid-thigh white tunics urged us to move faster. I don't mind telling you that I was surprised to find our first stop was the showers. The cadre told us to discard our clothes, every stitch, before entering. No one spoke, no chitchat or protests among the recruits. In fact, they all acted as though they were on Prozac. I looked this way and that, leaned out of line to see what was happening ahead, but I was the only one gawking.

Everyone disrobed like zombies, everyone but me. I am possessed of innate modesty, and I was reluctant to let go the last garment until a fellow in a tunic jerked it from my grip. I'm not used to parading around in the buff among strangers, and certainly not in church. The atmosphere in heaven, as you might imagine, is somewhat churchy.

You may not believe this, but the showers were coed. In their subdued state, none of the other recruits seemed to notice. I noticed. When I first glimpsed the plump young lady next to me, I noticed right away. I turned my shower to COLD and kept my eyes lifted in an attitude of prayer. "Pure thoughts, pure thoughts," I intoned to myself. It wouldn't have worked in life, and it didn't work then. I went into a crouch and duck-walked out the exit.

A tunic-clad cadre seized me by the arm and led me down the hall. "You have much to learn," he said, the disgust fairly dripping from his voice. "Shame, shame." I hung my head and followed, meek in my chastisement.

We entered a small room with REMEDIAL ATTI-TUDE CHAMBER above the door. There were no furnishings, just off-white walls and ceiling. The deep-pile white carpet beneath my bare feet felt nice, though. My escort turned to me. "You must think you are in Muslim heaven," he hissed. "You're not. This is Southern Baptist heaven. There are no seventy virgins for you here." His unfriendly demeanor seemed to mellow a bit. "Gate IV is for Southern Baptists, Gates I and II for Muslims, III for Episcopalians, and so forth." He explained further, "Each religion's followers go to a heaven that is exactly what that religion preached on earth. If abstinence was preached, abstinence is what you get. No matter that you sneaked about, indulged in strong drink and fleshly pursuits in life. Here you will eschew all worldly pleasures, as you were taught in Sunday school."

That seemed plain enough. "Is it too late to convert to Islam?" I inquired.

I swear his eyes bulged and his neck reddened. "You may not convert," he answered. Haughty. He seemed haughty to me. "There is only one direction you can go from here, and that is down." He emphasized that pronouncement with a southward thrust of his arm, like an umpire calling a third strike. "What you will do now is get back in line, take your shower and subdue your passions." I traipsed down the hall again, still buck-naked, but determined to succeed.

I failed. Lord knows I tried, but I failed again. Miserably. I had taken my place at the end of the shower line when something soft bumped against me from behind. I turned and started to scream, "Allah be praised," but caught myself in time. She was Salome, Delilah and Bathsheba all in one well-distributed package. She didn't look one damned bit like any Southern Baptist I'd ever known. She stood so close a Bicycle playing card couldn't have been inserted between us. I was led back to the Remedial Chamber, disgraced again.

After a thorough dressing down, the cadre gave me a three-strikes-and-you're-out warning. The thought of being consigned to the nether regions sobered me. I surely didn't want to chance going there. Better a known devil and all that. After some deep thinking, an idea came to me. I asked the cadre, "Do you have ice cubes?"

He blinked and then seemed to read my mind. "Follow me," he said. He led me to the cadre break-room and handed me a Zip-loc bag. There against the wall stood a side-by-side freezer/refrigerator, an Amana. Crystal chunks tumbled from the door dispenser. I took my two-pound icepack and headed once again for the showers.

Thank you, clever Amish in Iowa. If the ice supply held out, I was sure my days in heaven would be unnumbered.

That Bobby Earl

*K*arl, *in a blinding red rage, seized the stone vase and slammed it against Miriam's head. Chest heaving, he rolled her inert body, like a sack of garbage, over the boat rail and into the sea.*

Are you kidding me? This guy, Roche, is supposed to be such a great mystery writer and he ends a story like this. In disgust I layed the $24.95 book aside and stalked out of my apartment, craving boozey companionship.

I drove to Friendly Mae's, pulled into the parking lot and saw Bobby Earl's truck parked with his bass-boat hooked on behind. I'd have recognized his truck, even without the purple boat attached to it, just because of its hood ornament. No steer horns for Bobby Earl. No rearing chrome horse, either. He has a flower vase fastened to the hood, a tarnished, silver-plated, bug-spattered urn that belonged to his first wife. Then I made the connection between the boat, the vase and the book I'd just read. "You don't suppose," I asked myself, "that Bobby Earl's real name is Karl?" I chuckled at the idea as I entered the tavern.

Bobby Earl sat alone at a table, four or five Miller Lite empties in front of him, idly tapping his fingers to the Bob Wills tune coming from overhead speakers. He's twenty years younger than me, maybe in his late forties, but we socialize some. A tall fellow, maybe six-three or so, he favors Levi's jeans, the belt riding low under a stomach that looks like a concealed motorcycle helmet. Weathered the shade of worn-out boots from years of outdoor construction work, his long face is furrowed in deep creases, giving the benign appearance of a docile, slick-haired hound. He's always been a good listener, a quality I admire in people.

I went directly to the bar, picked up four beers from Mae and carried them to his table. "Hey, Bobby Earl," I said and set two bottles in front of him, reserving two for my own use.

"Hey," was his noncommittal response. He slid his chair back, stood and walked toward the restrooms at the back of the room. He pushed through the door of the Ladies' and right away came backing out, crab fashion, stared at the sign above the door like a rebuffed Basset, then moved along to the Men's. When he returned to the table he confided in a perfunctory drawl, "They was a woman in there." He tilted his current bottle up for a long drink and settled into contemplative silence. Bobby Earl's what you might call laconic.

I had to laugh at him, couldn't help it, and I started relating a similar experience I'd had. It was when I first got to Korea, back in '51. For the first three days, I was in transit— —Pusan to Taegu, Taegu to Yongdong-Po— —always in Army quarters with Western plumbing. At Yongdong-Po, where I was assigned to a railroad group and worked at a depot, the only latrine facility was Korean. The latrine building, a cut stone structure with slate roof, had been judiciously placed on the downwind side of the depot. A guide wasn't needed to find it, the aroma being what you might call aggressive. The latrine's interior layout consisted of six oblong slots in the concrete floor beginning near the entry door and extending some 18 feet along one wall— —no doors, no modesty panels. I hadn't been advised the facilities were co-ed.

On my first, somewhat hurried trip to this convenience, I stepped into the entryway and found myself in eye contact with an unblinking Korean woman squatted over the second slot. I froze for a moment. That is to say, the world stopped turning, and my brain was seized by generations of cultural inheritance warning me I should not be in this place. Her inscrutable Oriental face remained placidly unperturbed, expressing only ancient Eastern stoicism. I considered my options. Should I smile and say "Excuse me, ma'am" while I backed out the door? tip my hat? or just act like she wasn't there? The third action seemed best, me not speaking the language and all, and taking into account the urgency of my mission. I walked with studied nonchalance to the last slot of the row, putting as much space between us as the room's dimensions allowed.

I dropped my pants with as much aplomb as I could muster, and I was almost sure I heard a snicker. It could have been a throat-clearing— —the cultural barrier being what it is, I wasn't certain— —but this was something no male could ignore. From my crouched stance I took a furtive look to assess her state of mind. She appeared to be prayerfully studying the floor in front of her. If she was laughing, she concealed it well.

Then it came to me, the ecumenical aspects of our situation. The women's movement for equality was not prominent at the time, at least not in my mind, so I did not dwell on that at length, although the obvious, at-hand circumstances of share-and-share-alike were not lost on me. I was more attuned to the global significance of our condition— —hands across the sea, if you will. I took another look, measuring the distance between us, but elected not to reach out in noble gesture— —possibly another lost opportunity for greatness in my life.

Then things started to get complicated. Lieutenant Stillman walked in. I had been in the Army barely five months and did not as yet have a complete grasp of military protocol. In basic training when an officer entered the room you leaped to your feet, yelled "Ten-hut!" saluted and stood at attention until you were told, "At ease." I squirmed a bit over my slot, muscles tensed, sorting out the logistics of my anticipated move. The lieutenant said "Hi" and began unfastening his belt. There are times when procrastination pays real dividends.

First Lieutenant Stillman was built like a three-wire bale of hay stood on end. No more than five-eight in height, his weight had to be well in excess of 200 pounds. He took up a lot of space. Blond brush-cut hair, light enough to be the envy of Peggy Lee or Jean Harlowe, bristled from his scalp. Eyebrows of the same paleness seemed pasted on pink skin bright as a maidenly blush.

He eye-balled the empty slots as he began initial preparation for his planned activity. I was pretty sure he wouldn't take the end slot, between the woman and the far wall— —it would align him socially with her and leave me isolated, wondering if I'd neglected to brush my teeth. Besides, there just wasn't room for him over there. Since three empty slots remained between the woman and myself, it seemed logical a man of his breadth and intelligence would use the center one. But no, he chose the slot next to me.

I couldn't have been more uncomfortable if I was holding him on my lap. The very idea of this silver-barred, Occidental Buddha hunkering down beside me filled me with bowel-constricting panic. Squeezed into a suffocating posture between the lieutenant's bulk and the stone wall, I struggled to maintain my established position over the slot I had claimed. Military dignity, and whatever other kind I might once have possessed, were in the can, so to speak.

Korean restrooms did not provide toilet paper. The Army recognized these problems existed and thought-fully provided its members with little brown-wrapped packets, each containing about a week's worth of toi-let tissue. Fortunately, I carried mine in an accessible breast pocket of my fatigue jacket. In my cramped and contorted position, applying the tissue to its intended use required a few trial-and-error moves resulting in hopeful but unverified accomplishment.

I leaned forward and peered in front of the lieutenant to see if the woman had left the premises, not wanting to expose myself to further ridicule. She had silently de-parted, no doubt with hilarious stories about paki-tati Americans to recount over the hibachi, so I began the process of unwedging myself from the vise-like grip of the stone wall and Lieutenant Stillman's left haunch.

"Man, I couldn't wait to get out of that place," I summed-up for Bobby Earl. All during my recitation of events, he sat hunched over the table, silent as death, unsmiling and unmoving except to raise a bottle to his lips and tilt his head back every few seconds. Seven empties, like a squad of soldiers on smoke-break, stood in rout formation in front of him when I quit talking.

"Well, I swear," was his only comment.

I stared at him, trying to gauge his degree of intoxication while thoughts of boats and vases reappeared. "Your real name isn't Karl, is it?" I asked on the off chance the alcohol had sufficiently loosened his tongue.

His doggie eyes studied me briefly. "Hail no," he drawled with a hint of indignation, "It's Miriam." He rose unsteadily to his feet and made his way toward the restrooms.

Fore!

Cleon Horch, how did you ever get yourself into this mess? More to the point, how will you get yourself out? A grease monkey at Wal-Mart automotive center, you spend your weekdays under car hoods performing $19.95 oil-change specials. What made you aspire to the gentleman's game of golf?

Sure, your widowed aunt gave you Uncle Farris's mixed set of clubs. And sure, you've watched Tiger Woods hit straight and true down the fairway, chip into the hole from off the green. But golfers are people of breeding and refinement, Cleon. They're not your kind of folks. You know that, don't you? That's why you always play alone, why you decline invitations to join a threesome.

So you wait until late afternoon on this Saturday before going to the local links. The crowd has thinned, the first fairway stretches open and inviting. Shoulder muscles bunched, you drive the ball in a magnificent high arc, and it slices, slices, slices... out of bounds deep into the woods. It was a brand new ball, too.

You whistle a few bars of "My Window Faces South" while you walk to the point your ball entered the trees. You drop the bag off the fairway and crawl through the barbed-wire fence, eight-iron in hand in case a snake is encountered. The club comes into use parting blackberry vines and pushing aside low-hanging pine branches.

Forty yards into the dense growth you discover a man's body. He lies facedown on a cushion of pine needles, shirt bunched around his waist, trousers around his knees.

You recognize Judge Wilburn, retired from the superior court bench of Bixford County. The judge is in his 80's, an avid golfer, but his presence here is puzzling. Then your quick mind assimilates the facts. A pile of fresh human excrement with green flies swirling about, pants down... The judge must have been taking a dump and had a heart attack.

But wait. Less than three club-lengths from the body you spot a golf ball. When examined, there's no doubt whose ball it is. It now has a smile in the cover, but it's your ball, Cleon. Could it be...? You take a closer look at the judge. Sure enough, there's a goose egg bump on the back of his head. It doesn't say Max-Fli, but it has dimples.

You leap to your feet as though spring-loaded. A wide-eyed 360-degree sweep reveals no witnesses. This deplorable situation could spell trouble. You don't want to be seen with the judge, but you can't just walk away and leave him here. You pull the body into a sitting position and, not wanting to leave the eight-iron behind, stick it shaft-first down the judge's shirt collar. Hoisted into place, you hold his wrists firmly and head for the fairway, the judge riding piggyback.

But hold on a minute, Cleon. Image has never been foremost among your concerns, but you are a thoughtful person. Might it not be more seemly if the judge's trousers were in place? From the rear your cargo appears to be twin loaves of light bread separated by a leather-bound club grip. The stainless steel face of the pitching niblick gleams above the judge's distended collar. You unload your burden, tug, zip and belt him, a process made difficult because you neglected to first pull his shorts up.

At the fence you take stock of your surroundings. The sun is low over the clubhouse. Cloud-cover in the west spreads gloom over all. Darkness is not far off, and can you believe it, two guys in a golf cart are making their way toward the first tee.

You are panicked. It shows in your eyes. You stuff the judge under the fence, crawl through and reload. A brisk dogtrot brings you to the first green after 150 yards of huffing and puffing. Breathless and frightened of being discovered, you lay the judge in a bunker. Only one solution comes to mind. You begin scooping sand onto the body.

Decency prevails and you leave the head uncovered until last. When the first spray of sand hits his face the judge's eyes pop open.

"Judas priest," he exclaims.

You fall away, slack-mouth astounded. He uncovers an arm and paws at his face, spits grit from his mouth and sits erect. With awkward, arthritic dignity he extracts the eight-iron from his shirt, examines it at length and tosses it aside.

He casts about in bewilderment at the bunker, at the green, at you. He gingerly touches the back of his head. Then, almost in spasm, he claws at his crotch in obvious discomfort. He writhes in the sand, both hands groping and tugging, then looks back and demands, "What the hell have you done to me?"

Hurt by the judge's tone, Cleon, you tell him the God's-honest-truth. "I was just tryin' to help, Your Honor."

The judge struggles to his feet. "I don't believe I could survive any more of your help, Boy. If the law permitted, I'd have you caned for this. Now stay away from me." He begins walking toward the clubhouse, shaking first one leg and then the other to dislodge sand.

You trot to catch up, make one last effort at reconciliation. "Honest, Your Honor, I never meant no harm."

The judge turns and shakes a fist. "Keep away from me, Boy. You hear?" He resumes walking, then over his shoulder shouts, "Cretin."

Dejected, you trail at a distance until you come to your clubs lying next to the fence. You study them for a long moment then pick up the bag and heave it into the woods. You did the right thing, Cleon.

Here's to EAP

'Twas moonshine a-simmer,
O'er a midnight fire;
Music, sweet music,
Notes plucked from a lyre.
Sour mash in its goodness
Will forfeit the prize
Of joy and good will
Before the sunrise.
I raised a sip,
Liquor to lip;
Too raw- too raw for me-
Three days in a jug,
Corked tight and snug,
Will make three-star, you see.
Sturdy brown crock,
Distill, unlock
Thine essence and set it free;
Transform it to silk,
Like mother's milk,
The gift of the Gods it endue.
Its praises in song
I'll sing ere long,
An ode to heavenly brew.

Tumbleweed

Pigs are noisy animals. They don't smell too good either. I watched the farm truck make a left at the intersection and disappear with its squealing cargo. "This is far as I go," the driver told me when he let me out. He'd picked me up about thirty miles back. I started hoofing it.

Most of an hour later I came to a highway sign. Rusted bullet holes punctuated REMORSE 3. An arrow pointed to the right. My stomach reminded me of the breakfast I'd missed. I took the gravel road in the hope of finding a town and a meal. I didn't know if I was in Oklahoma or Kansas. Had to be one or the other. No matter, I began mulling over my situation.

Divorce is hard. We never had much in the three years we were married, but Phyllis took most of it, including the car and the trailer. "Cus," she said. My name's Custis, but most folks call me Cus. "You haven't grown. You're still the same little boy you always were." Can't fool old Phyllis. She had me dead to rights. I never did work well in double harness anyway.

I didn't see any need of hanging around. No property. Unemployment checks about to run out. I hit the road and hitchhiked across three states. Now here I was in Kansas. Or Oklahoma.

The road rose and fell through rolling countryside. Lines of trees marked watercourses. Farmsteads a half-mile or mile apart dotted the expanse. At the top of a rise I could see Remorse, a gathering of a couple of dozen buildings. I picked up the pace for the remaining quarter-mile.

Shady lawns and occasional picket fences lined the road. No one in sight except a sleeping dog. I spotted a grocery store with gas pumps in front. Inside, the smell of onions and potatoes greeted me. An open sack of each stood next to the door. A middle-aged man wearing a green apron stood watching two elderly gents play dominos.

The grocer turned as I entered. "Help you with anything, Mister?" He was a round-faced friendly fellow. Reminded me of a favorite uncle.

"Yes, sir. I need something to eat. Bread and meat and milk'll do fine."

He walked toward the counter. "I make a good sandwich for a dollar, drink is extra." I agreed, and he busied himself putting my meal together.

I sat at the end of the domino table and tore into my sandwich. The grocer remained standing at my shoulder. "Are you a single man?" he inquired. I nodded yes and continued feeding. "Think he'll do?" he asked the two men. They both glanced at me and nodded.

"What this is about," he said to me, "is we have a town festival every year or two, and we'd like you to be our guest of honor."

I sure wasn't on any schedule, but Remorse didn't seem to have any bright lights that would make a stranger want to hang around long. As soon as I could swallow I asked him, "When is this festival?"

"Starts this evening an hour before sundown."

What the heck? I could sleep under a tree and be on my way early tomorrow. "Sure, I don't mind. Thanks for the invitation."

He took a pad of paper and a ballpoint out of his pocket. "I need your full name and date of birth, if you don't mind."

"Custis Laverne Duckworth," I told him and then added my birth date.

The grocer looked at his watch. "Better start rounding folks up," he told the domino players. They scooted their chairs back and silently went out the door. He treated me to another glass of milk and occupied himself with a feather duster for a while. "Well, we don't want to be late," he said, removing his apron. "Let's go."

We got into a pickup truck parked outside and drove around a field adjacent to the town. A sizeable group of people gathered in the shade of an oak grove. He parked the truck under a giant tree, got out and let the tailgate down. He stepped up into the bed and motioned for me to follow. Two husky young men from the crowd joined us.

"Folks, I'd like you to meet our guest of honor, Custis Duckworth." He turned to me. "Mr. Duckworth, what this is about is whenever we have some spinsters in our town we like to help them find a marriage partner." Red flags went up. About that time the two men next to me each took a firm grip on an arm.

"Hold on. What are you doing?" I struggled some, but they were stout boys.

"Will the ladies please step forward?" Three young women lined up in front of the tailgate. "The way this works, Mr. Duckworth, is you'll choose one of these ladies and then an hour before sundown we'll hang you. If the woman of your choice can hold you up until the sun goes down the two of you will be joined in holy wedlock. Otherwise, we wish you better luck next time."

Was he serious? The two men tied my hands behind me, roped my feet together. A noose was tossed over a limb and placed around my neck. If he wasn't serious he sure had me fooled.

"The first lady is Verniece." A clock-stopper if I ever saw one. "Second is Glorianna." A man could get real interested in this one. "The third is Hilda." If she was a male she'd have football scholarship offers from the Sooners and the Jayhawks. "It's almost time, Mr. Duckworth. Make your choice."

What I wanted to do was scream for help. Instead I began appraising the eager females. Aside from her looks, Verniece was a bit on the frail side. I doubted her skinny arms and legs could support me.

A man might be willing to die in the arms of buxom Glorianna. I made a mental check mark beside her name.

One glance at Hilda and I almost spoke for Glorianna. But then my good sense kicked in. I decided that Hilda was the one most likely to still be on her feet at sundown. She looked like she could push a plow with one hand. "Hilda," I announced.

The two muscle guys lifted me and set me upright on the tailgate. The grocer instructed Hilda to hold me. He then hopped down and drove the pickup forward, leaving me in Hilda's grasp. She staggered in a half circle with her face buried in my stomach until she achieved balance.

Do you have any idea how slow the sun moves? I tried not to think about it and craned my neck, seeking relief from the rope's pressure. You'd think they'd use cotton or nylon, something smooth, instead of sisal. "Hang in there, Hilda," I urged periodically.

I opened my eyes and saw only red. Was I dead? Hallucinating? No, it was the blessed sun under the horizon, the most beautiful sunset I ever witnessed. The grocer backed the truck up, and Hilda set my feet on the tailgate.

The grocer's helpers untied me and removed the noose from my neck. They jumped down and, with considerable effort, boosted Hilda onto the truck bed causing the left-side springs to bottom-out.

The grocer, apparently a jack-of-all-trades, intoned, "Dearly beloved, we are gathered here to join this man and this…"

I felt the sudden and immediate need of exercise. I leaped over the side and hit the ground at a gallop. Angry shouts and the noise of pursuit provided incentive. Nothing ever felt so good as the turf rising to meet my feet, the wind singing in my ears. I lost them on a wooded hillside and eased into a dogtrot.

By dark I'd slowed to a walk to avoid a collision with a tree or fence. Exhausted, I bedded down under a spreading elm and settled into untroubled sleep.

I woke to the sound of tires singing on pavement. I sat up in time to see a pickup disappear around a bend in a road not 50 feet from where I'd slept. Bird song and squirrel chatter accompanied me as I set out walking the narrow blacktop.

In less than an hour I came to the outskirts of town. RUEFUL, the sign said. I walked past a Sinclair station and soon came to a small grocery store. The familiar smell of potatoes and onions greeted my entrance. Two men sat at a table playing gin rummy.

A sturdy fellow in a green apron read a newspaper behind the counter. I selected a fried apple pie from a rack and got a pint container of milk from the cold box. When I handed money to the grocer he silently rang up the sale then asked, "Are you a single man?"

Seemed like I'd been down this road before. I took my change from him and cheerfully lied, "No, sir. Happily married." I didn't let the door hit me on the way out.

Someday I hope I can afford a better class of transportation. Beggars can't be too choosy, I guess. I rode in a rusted pickup bed on the passenger side. "There ain't enough room in the cab," the skinny old rancher said when he'd stopped for me ten miles back. I couldn't help noticing there was plenty of room for the saddle in the seat beside him.

In the truck bed opposite me was one of those black-and-gray-spotted Australian cow dogs. Smelled like dead rabbit. Bob-tailed he was and standoffish. Every time I shifted position he turned his head toward me and curled an upper lip. What with keeping an eye on the dog and holding my hat on my head I had my hands full.

I'd hitchhiked my way down from the Oklahoma-Kansas border area after an unfortunate experience with the locals up that way. I needed to find a place to hang my hat for a while, get a job and get back on my feet—financially speaking, that is. Lord knows I'd worn out plenty of shoe leather the last few days. I thought I'd give Texas a try.

The pickup squealed to a stop at a crossroads. "This is far as you go," the rancher informed me. I hopped over the side, not unhappy to part company with that surly dog. The old man turned to the right on a gravel road, a rooster-tail of dust in his wake. A sign pointing the other way read AMICABLE 2. That's the way I went, hoping to find a meal.

A half-hour walk brought me to the outskirts of town. Next to a 20-acre field of portable drilling rigs, racks of drill-stem and steel vats the size of river barges a fair was in progress. BLIND PETE COUNTY FAIR, the overhead canvas sign read. Behind a multi-colored kiddy merry-go-round I spotted a foot-long hotdog stand. I wasn't used to paying $2 for a hotdog, but they looked filling. Smelled good, too. The man in the booth loaded it up with chopped onion, pickle relish and mustard. I added a line of catsup the length of the bun.

"You want to earn some money?" I'd just taken the first bite when this fella behind me spoke. I turned to be sure he was talking to me. I suppose he could tell from the look of my clothes that I might respond to the mention of money. "My name's Buster Carstairs. I'm the fair manager." He stuck his hand out.

I swallowed, changed hands with the hotdog, licked catsup off my finger and shook with him. "I'm Custis Duckworth. Pleased to meet you, Mr. Carstairs."

"I need a judge for one of the fair events." He looked at his watch. "The contest starts in about a half-hour." I guess he noticed me hesitate. "Pays $30," he added.

"Why can't you get somebody local to do it?" I couldn't figure why he'd picked me, a stranger.

Carstairs came up to about my shoulder, round face with sweat running down. He mopped his brow with a dingy handkerchief. "Folks around here don't want the job. Can't pay 'em to do it."

"Why's that, Mr. Carstairs? What kind of a contest is it?"

He chuckled and leaned toward me in a conspiratorial way. "It's a ugly baby contest. We usually try to get a outsider to do the judging." Well that explained a lot.

A recent divorce had separated me from most of my worldly goods. Shoot, I needed the money, so why not give it a try? "I'll do it, Mr. Carstairs."

I never had much to do with babies. They all demanded a lot of attention without showing much gratitude. A litter of pups had more personality.

Two rows of eight chairs atop a raised platform seated the contestants. With an age limit of one year, each entrant sat on its mother's lap. Some cried, some sucked on bottles, some slept and some just stared goggle-eyed. Mr. Carstairs introduced me then continued. "This year's winner will receive a certificate for $150 worth of merchandise at Grafton's Feed and Grocery. Let the judging begin."

I stepped over and stood in front of contestant #1. What I saw caused my eyes to shut tight, face squeezed up like I'd just drank castor oil. Not the baby—I was looking at its mother. Whew! I'd sure enough earn my money on this job.

I tried to make an honest effort. It wasn't easy because there were several truly unattractive young ones in the group, not to mention the older ones. I finally awarded the certificate to #12, a child who, I kid you not, drew a painfully short straw on looks. I hoped I wasn't expected to kiss the winner.

"Fraud!" a mother yelled. "How much did she pay you?" "It's fixed, it's fixed." The ladies got testier by the minute. Fists were raised, angry threats shouted.

I looked around in a panic for escape. Carstairs stood off to one side of the audience, arms folded over his belly, a smirk across his face. I jumped off the platform and raced toward him. He handed me the $30, like passing a baton in a relay race, as I went past. "Better get out of town, Duckworth," he yelled to my back. The man was laughing at me.

I made it back to the main highway in quick time, out of breath and looking over my shoulder. I held my thumb up to an approaching car. An aging Toyota sedan with a man, a woman and five stair-step kids stopped beside me. "Get in, neighbor," the man invited.

I opened the rear door and looked for a place to sit. "You'll have to hold Grainger on your lap, I expect," the driver offered. "You don't mind, do you?"

I minded a-plenty. "No, I don't mind." I hoisted the two-year-old boy to my lap and felt a lump the size of my fist in his Huggies. I cracked the window to let in fresh air and leaned my head in that direction. Grainger, bless him, groped my face and chin with sticky fingers. I really wished I could afford better transportation.

❊ ❊ ❊

Nearly dark. I stood under an overpass, thumb held up toward approaching headlights. After an unproductive day hitchhiking I was tired, tired and hungry. I'd been in east Texas a few days before deciding to head west.

A car slowed and braked to a stop 100 feet past me, seventy-something Cadillac, bad muffler, power-steering belt screeching. I ran up to the back door and climbed in. Right away I smelled whiskey. The dome light revealed a man in a dirty cowboy hat behind the wheel, thick neck, needed a shave. A gum-chewing blonde woman sat on the passenger side, up-do, blue plastic earrings the size of bracelets. The driver looked over his shoulder at me until I closed the door. "Jim Bob's the name. I can take you far as Amarillo." He didn't introduce the woman.

"Sure do appreciate you, Jim Bob. My name's Custis."

The woman giggled. "That's a right pretty name," she said, all smiley like.

Jim Bob said, "Lo-rene." Said it with a kind of warning growl. He tipped a pint bottle to his lips, corked it and stuck it down beside him. He tromped on the gas pedal, took the passing lane and stayed in it.

I tried to settle in, maybe get some sleep. I leaned against the driver's side, legs across the seat, and closed my eyes. "You want some chicken?" The woman was looking over the seat back, a red and white KFC box in her hand. "Lorene, what are you doin'?" Jim Bob demanded.

"I'm just askin' him if he wants this leftover chicken is all. What's wrong with you, Jim Bob?"

She reached the box toward me and I took it. "Thank you, Ma'am." An extra-crispy cold wing and leg greeted me. Half starved, I tore right into them.

"You're welcome, Custis," she replied with another giggle.

"Lorene, I'm tellin' you right now, stop flirtin' with that there road bum." He had me figured about right, but his tone of voice was harsh, uncalled for. I kept right on eating, although I thought Jim Bob might bear watching. He seemed to get worked-up easy. Things settled down by the time I finished the chicken. I leaned back and closed my eyes. It wasn't thirty seconds before Jim Bob said, "You always have to do that, don't you?"

"Do what, Jim Bob, do what?" Sounded like Lorene was getting her back up.

"You know what, Lorene. You just got to flirt with every scumbag that comes along. Well, I ain't goin' to put up with it no longer. You got that?" It was getting raucous up there in the front seat. Why couldn't they just let a man sleep? Lorene tuned the radio to a C&W music station. Loud. Guitars and nasal singing.

The radio snapped off. "You hear me good, Lorene. You flirt with that bum one more time, I'll kill both of you." My eyes popped open.

Now that sleep was out of the question I paid closer attention to Jim Bob. He took another hit on the bottle. Next thing I knew he was steering with his knees and jamming a clip into the butt of some kind of semi-automatic pistol. I thought about jumping, but we must have been doing seventy-five.

I sat up straight. "Jim Bob, I sure don't want to cause any trouble. Why don't you just stop and let me out? Any place along here'll be fine." The man was beginning to worry me. He worked the slide, chambering a round.

"I'm on to you, Bud. I know your kind. A man gives you a lift and right away you start makin' a play for his woman." What had I done? What had I said? It was plain that Jim Bob wasn't a man of reason.

"Honest, Jim Bob." I hated the way my voice shook. "Honest, I didn't have anything like that in mind. If you'll just let me out…"

He slammed on the brakes. We skidded to a stop on the shoulder next to the median. "Get out of the car," he ordered. I opened the door and couldn't help noticing that he opened his. We both stood outside, separated by the rear door standing open.

He thumbed the safety off. "I'm goin' to give you a runnin'…" I never knew I could accelerate like that. "…head start." I was crossing the traffic lane angling back the way we'd come when he fired. If he'd shot the whole clip I couldn't have gone any faster.

I coasted to a stop after I heard the car door slam and the muffler roar. Talk about your Good Samaritans, that old boy took the cake. Beat anything I ever saw.

Full dark now. I'd walked a good while when a 3/4–ton Chevy truck stopped. Furniture piled in the back, chairs and such. The driver got out and walked behind the truck toward me. "Howdy, Bud. Would you mind driving us on in to Amarillo? I'm plumb tired, about to go to sleep. I'd look on it as a favor if you would." Seemed like a nice enough fella.

"Sure. Glad to do it." If you can't help your fellow man, who can you help? I got behind the wheel and noticed a woman on the far end of the seat. "Evenin', Ma'am." I always try to be polite with people. The driver got in and scooted her to the middle.

Nice-handling truck. I got it up to road speed and settled into a comfortable position. The driver had his head leaned against the cab in a sleeping position. First thing I knew the woman laid a hand on my knee.

I almost wrecked the truck. I guess that's what woke the man. "Eula Faye, quit that if you know what's good for you." Snarly voice, not at all like he was before. She

Loose Ends

jerked her hand back. "You already caused me to kill one man. Don't make me have to do that again."

I squeezed over against the door and started a desperate watch for mileage signs to Amarillo. I sure hoped Eula Faye had learned her lesson.

I was footloose, you might say, in Amarillo. I decided to abandon Interstate travel for a while, it being too chancy for my taste. I walked along a state route a ways kicking beer cans in the grass without getting a ride. A convenience store attracted my attention, coffee and a cinnamon roll being on my mind. I headed for the entry.

Two boys, teenagers I'd guess, went in ahead of me. Stringy hair, acne, blue bandanas around their necks, both of them wore greasy caps on their heads. Could pass for twins. I followed them inside and went to the coffee stand. "This is a hold-up." Curious, I turned around.

The boys had pulled the bandanas up over their noses. One of them held a wood-handled six-shooter pistol on the cashier. Seemed like just about everybody in Texas carried a gun nowadays. They either didn't know or didn't care that they'd been on camera since they came through the door. I could see all of us on the wall monitor behind the cash register, the scowling woman cashier, the two boys and me. I never did take a good picture.

The kid with the gun waved it at the cashier. "Put all the money in a paper sack," he ordered. The cylinder flopped open. A bullet dropped to the floor, bounced and rolled. He thumbed the cylinder closed, and it immediately fell open again. This time he kept his thumb on it.

The unarmed one found some cardboard boxes behind the counter and filled one with cigarette cartons. "Get something to eat," the pistol holder told him. He took an empty box and raked packaged items off the shelf, Twinkies, Moon Pies, whatever was in front of him. "We need some beer." He took an empty carton to the cooler and filled it with six-packs of Busch. "Let's get out of here."

Six-gun picked up the Twinkies, still holding his thumb on the pistol. "I can't carry both of these boxes," the kid toting the beer told him.

Six-gun motioned to me. "Hey you, Bud." My name's not Bud, it's Custis. I don't like for people to call me Bud. "Pick up the cigarettes," he ordered.

"But I don't smoke." It sounded lame, even to me.

"I ain't askin' you to smoke 'em, Dummy. Just carry 'em out to the car." Smart-mouthed kid. I think I liked Bud better than Dummy.

We loaded the three cartons into the back of a blue Ford Escort that had seen its best days. It was parked next to the gas pumps. Probably stole the gas, too. I would have got their license number if there'd been a tag. They left the parking lot and took the state route south.

I hadn't no more than got back inside when a police car pulled in. Blue lights flashing. Two city cops, shirts tight over their bellies. I went to the coffee stand while the cashier related the facts. She seemed extra calm to me. Probably been robbed more than once. One cop reported the blue Escort on a hand-held radio.

The cashier, mean little eyes, hair growth on her upper lip, leaned past the cop taking notes. She looked and pointed at me. "He helped them." I almost dropped my coffee. My mouth, half full of cinnamon roll, gaped in disbelief.

A cop took me by the arm. "Y'all better come with us." We hadn't got to the door when the cashier said, "He ain't paid for his coffee and roll yet." I dug money out of my pocket and waited for the change.

Why did misfortune always smile on me? If somebody wrote it in a book nobody would believe it.

I was the sole occupant of the holding cell. After they watched the security tape the cops began to lose interest in me. If I'd been able to give them a home address they might have turned me loose. I cooled my heels while they searched for outstanding wants and warrants.

It wasn't long before two cops came in leading the boys. Hands cuffed behind their backs. Moon Pie crumbs in the corner of one's mouth, on his shirt. The cops ushered them into my cell.

"Well, if it ain't the dummy. Ha-ha-ha." It was the brains of the outfit, the guy who'd held the gun. "What they got you for?"

"Just visiting," I told him. "I'll be long gone while you two are still sitting here."

"Duckworth." A man in a suit peered through the bars at me. "I'm Detective Arsenio." Nice suit. Clark Gable mustache. "You're going to be our guest for a while. We have to hold you as a material witness since you don't have a permanent address."

"Ha-ha-ha." Let him laugh. It wasn't like I was on a schedule.

Four or five days later, I kind of lost track, the boys took a plea, and I was on my way again. That same convenience store loomed in front of me. Bad as I hated to go back in that place, I headed for the entrance. That was a sure enough tasty cinnamon roll I'd had before, and my stomach was talking to me.

The door flew open and a woman carrying a cardboard box under her arm ran into me. Paper sack setting on top. What looked like a .22 pistol in her right hand. The box and the sack fell to the blacktop.

"Watch where you're going, Dummy," she snarled. Nice looking lady, other than that. Dark hair. Brown eyes. She grabbed the paper sack. "Pick up the box, Dummy, and carry it to the car." She opened the door, and I slid the box onto the back seat of the brown Buick Special. She didn't even say, "Thank you." Nice looking car. I memorized her license number.

Inside, I enjoyed my coffee and cinnamon roll while the same clerk glared at me. We waited in silence for the cops to arrive. I sure hoped that female bandit would cop a plea.

❄   ❄   ❄

There's a lot of sky over west Texas with not much of interest under it. I'd hitchhiked down a state highway, gladly leaving the hazards of interstate travel behind. The town of Eartick fit the lack-of-interest description—one dusty street with dusty pickups parked in front of dusty buildings. But I welcomed habitation after all the emptiness.

Being well past lunchtime, I'd gone into the only grocery store and interrupted the proprietor's checker game to buy a snack. I returned to the highway, a carton of milk in one hand and a fried apple pie in the other. The pie, stale but filling, and the milk, cold and delicious, helped fill the void in my stomach.

A Jeep pickup stopped beside me. I hadn't seen one in years. It might have been the last one in America not on blocks, maybe older than I was. In the truck bed a couple of sacks of cottonseed cake and a salt block suggested cattle rancher. "Hop in, Pilgrim," a female voice invited. I tossed the empty milk carton away and opened the door.

The driver, a store blonde with one of those shel-lacked-in-place beehive hair-dos, patted the passenger seat, inviting me to enter. I thought that hairstyle had gone out of fashion, but then I don't really keep up with that sort of thing.

I guessed her at mid to late thirties. Had those little age-lines around her mouth and eyes. She wore jeans and boots and a halter that was under considerable stress in its supporting role. Friendly smile. "Where 'bouts you headed?" She had a kind of chirpy voice, musical but with nasal tendencies.

"Nowhere in particular, Ma'am. I'm just out seeing the world."

She threw her head back and let out a raucous bray of laughter. "You taken a wrong turn, Bud. The world is back that-a-way." She jerked her thumb over her shoulder. "What on earth brings you to this here part of Texas?" She crammed the gearshift into low and let out the clutch.

I wasn't sure I knew the answer to that myself, but I gave her a brief overview of my loss of assets in a recent divorce. "There wasn't anything left for me at home, so I hit the road."

"Well bless your heart," she responded, the words in heavy syrup. "My name's Twila, what's yours?" High gear had us tooling along the blacktop at 45.

"Custis," I told her, "Custis Duckworth."

"That's a right poetic name, Custis." At least she didn't laugh. We rode in silence for a few seconds before she said, "Tell you what, Custis, you look like a man who could use a home-cooked meal. How does that sound?"

It sounded like heaven on earth. "It sounds fine, but I don't want to be any trouble."

"Shoot. No trouble a-tall. You just relax yourself, Custis. You're in good hands with ol' Twila." I wasn't real sure what she meant by that.

After turning off the highway onto a gravel road for a mile or so, Twila pulled into a dirt yard beside a board-and-batten wind and sun-dried house. A desolate barn in the distance canted with the prevailing wind. "This here is it," she said, "the old homestead." Mixed-breed cattle grazed in a pasture beyond four strands of barbed wire.

"You live here by yourself?"

"I sure enough do, ever since my second husband took off with his tail between his legs. He's a flutist for the Amarillo Symphony. I guess he decided I was too much woman for him, so he taken up the flute to console hisself." She had herself another braying laugh.

She led the way up the back steps, through a service porch and into the kitchen. "While I fix supper, Custis, you likely want to clean up some. I don't mind telling you you're a little on the rank side. There's a shower through that door yonder. I'll throw your clothes in the washer while you're doing that. You can just drop 'em right here, or if you're the bashful kind just throw 'em out the bathroom door." That's what I opted to do.

Nothing makes you feel better when you're on the road than a long hot shower. I got all the grit out of my hair and hide and soaked until the water started to cool. I wrapped a towel around me and stuck my head out the door. "How are my clothes coming?" Smells from the kitchen produced stomach rumbles. Twila had something cooking that smelled a lot like fried chicken.

"Clothes'll be done in a minute, Custis. Step on out here and let me get a look at you." Towel around my waist, I walked hesitantly into the kitchen. "Lord, you look good enough to eat." She brayed that laugh again. "But I reckon I better save you for dessert."

After my clothes dried and I'd dressed we sat down to the best meal I'd had since my mama cooked for me — pan-fried chicken, potatoes and gravy and corn on the cob. Mm-m, mm-m. "Time for dessert," she declared.

"Twila," I told her, "I am stuffed. I don't have room for another bite."

She looked at me like a duck eyeing a Junebug. "You'll have room for this. C'mon, we'll leave the dishes 'til later." She stood and pulled me to my feet. At her bedroom door she said, "Just give me a minute to get things ready." My heart pumped with a life of its own. I had more than a passing interest in whatever she was doing on the other side of the door. "Ready," she chirped. Me too.

Big smile. Hungry look. She stood birth naked with hands on hips, a bee-hived goddess. When my gaze drifted down I noticed she still wore boots and that she'd strapped roweled spurs on them. Next I saw the restraints, buckled straps, one on each bedpost. On the nightstand next to the bed stood an open box of plastic gloves and a half-pound jar of petroleum jelly. A braided leather quirt and what looked like an electric curling iron hung on the wall. The urgency I'd felt melted into a need for hasty departure.

The bedroom windows were opened for cross-ventilation. I took a screen with me on the way out, but I remembered my manners. "Thanks for supper," I called over my shoulder. No wonder her second husband taken up the flute.

❊ ❊ ❊

I was in high spirits this spring morning. Sun so bright it nearly blinded me, fields green with lush grass. Texas Panhandle after April rains. I'd been walking an hour or more, rides being scarce in these parts. Hitchhiking is a poor man's transportation and tiresome, but this day I didn't mind. I whistled a nameless tune while I walked.

Up ahead a man sat on a low bridge rail. He lifted an apple to his mouth and took a bite. When I came closer I saw it wasn't a man but a boy. And he wasn't eating an apple. It was a big onion. I stopped a few feet away, staring, before he looked at me for the first time.

"What?" he said, "You never seen no onion before?" Mouthy kid. I'd guess him at no more than twelve or maybe thirteen. Barefoot. Dirty jeans and blue shirt with the tail hanging out. Hair the color of dried foxtail stuck out under a frayed straw hat. He'd shoved the hat to the back of his head, cocky like.

I sat down on the rail leaving a yard of space between us. "I've seen onions before, but I don't make a habit of eating them like apples. Is that all you have to eat?"

He swallowed and gave me a hard glance. "Why? You writin' a book?"

I sighed and shook my head. "Don't act so tough.

There's a town a couple of miles ahead, and I thought I'd offer to buy you a meal if you're hungry."

He scooted away from me a foot or so. "You ain't one of them pre-verts are you? 'Cause if you are I don't want nothin' to do with you."

I laughed. "No, I'm not a 'pre-vert'. What's your name, tough guy?"

He hesitated, eyed me over good before he answered. "Name's Durwood, if it's anything to you."

I stood and headed up the highway. "I'm going to have me some ham and eggs, Durwood," I called over my shoulder. "If you want some you can come with me." I heard his bare feet slapping the pavement until he caught up. He reeked with onion.

"What's your name?" he asked from beside me.

"Custis," I told him, "if it's anything to you." He didn't respond. "Where you from, Durwood?"

"Oh, uh, from Dallas. I live in Dallas." He barely came up to my shoulder, and he had to stretch his legs to keep up the pace.

"You're a long way from home. What brings you out this way."

"Well, I'll tell you. See, my daddy's a rich man, richer than Ross Perot. We live in a great big old house, so big it hangs over the lot lines all around. Has a twelve-car garage to hold all the automobiles my daddy owns. Maids and butlers and such all over the place. I just wanted to get away from all that for a while. You know what I mean?"

He looked serious, like he expected me to believe him. "Yeah, I know what you mean, Durwood. Wealth can be a real burden on a fella." I couldn't help laughing at the little liar. "If your daddy's so rich how come you don't have money for food?"

He didn't bat an eye. "A gang of thieves jumped me. Took everything I own, even my shoes. I tried to fight 'em off, but there was just too many of 'em." He glanced at me to see if I was paying attention. "That's why I'm wearin' these here old clothes. At home I don't wear nothin' but silk suits."

The town of Grateful spread like impetigo on the face of the prairie, its development arrested decades ago. Several pickups occupied the hard-packed dirt parking area in front of Sip and Ovella's Café. "How about we wash-up first, Durwood?" I suggested. He cast a withering glance at me like the concept was foreign to him. But he followed me into the men's room and reluctantly dashed water over his face and arms.

We claimed a booth by the front window and ordered breakfast from a plump and chirpy waitress. Nametag read, Polly. "Here you go, gents," she gushed a few minutes later. "Enjoy yourselfs."

Durwood's hands shook, could hardly find his mouth with his fork. Never lifted his face from the plate for five minutes. He gorged himself, egg-yolk trickling from the corner of his mouth. "Um-um, that sure was good," he said while mopping up the last traces with a biscuit.

I couldn't resist prodding him a bit. "Better than onion, I'll bet."

"You got that right." He sat back against the booth. "A man hadn't ought to face the day without a little hog grease in him," he observed.

I finished eating and gave Polly some money. "Well, Durwood, I guess this is where you and me part company."

"What are you talkin' about?" Alarm, like an animal startled, widened his eyes.

I gave him my most serious look. "I can't afford to take care of you, Durwood. You need to go home." I laid a dollar bill in front of him. "Here's money for a phone call. Ring up your daddy and have him send the chauffeur for you." His gaze dropped and his body slumped, defeated.

I stepped out of the booth. "It's been nice meeting you, Durwood. Take care." I went out the door and headed for the highway.

Thirty minutes later the slap-slap of bare feet sounded behind me. He came even with me, matched my gait and walked in silence. I was tempted to throw rocks and chase him off like a stray dog, but I didn't.

Before noon the sky darkened. Thunder growled, and lightning flashed to the west of us. "We're about to get wet if we don't find shelter somewhere." A few big drops made dark spatters on the blacktop.

Somebody up there must have liked us, because right about then I spotted a vacant barn in a field up ahead. The rain came down, serious like. "Let's go." The two of us ran like the devil himself was after us and entered the barn just partly wet. We lay on musty straw and listened to hail and rain rattle the sheet metal roof.

Durwood scooted closer to me. "This here old barn won't last a minute in a tornado," he said, eyes wide and face pale. "My family has a history with tornados, they're always looking for us." He sat upright. "One hit our house one time and left Mama setting on a tree limb with a 40-pound shoat in her lap. We never did figure where the pig came from, but he followed Mama around like a pup after that." Talking, lying, seemed to defeat his fear. He continued. "One hit our chicken house, and it snowed feathers for a week after." He grew quiet as the storm lessened and became a steady rain.

He turned to face me. "Custis." It was the first time he'd spoke my name. "Custis, I ain't been altogether truthful with you." No kidding. "I don't really live in Dallas and my daddy ain't rich. I don't even have a daddy." His hands fidgeted like the truth was hard for him to deal with. "I run away from home day before yesterday. Now I'm on my way back. I live in Stokes, the next town up the road. My mama's going to be worried about me."

Stokes, Texas looked a lot like Grateful, Texas, forlorn under the vast expanse of sky. We walked together down a muddy street to a modest house with flower boxes full of geranium blooms. A woman with disheveled hair and drawn face rushed out to meet us. She cuffed Durwood's head affectionately before embracing him. I stood awkwardly as silent tears wet her cheeks. She wiped her eyes with her apron before asking me, "Won't you come in?"

"Thank you, Ma'am, but I need to be on my way." I turned toward the highway.

I heard Durwood excitedly tell her, "Mama, me and Custis was caught in a tornado, right in the middle of it. You should've seen it. Limbs flyin' everywhere, lightnin' hittin' all around us, it was a sight."

The truth shall set you free.

❅   ❅   ❅

I had money in my pocket. I'd filled in for a week on a crew that worked its way north, Texas to Montana, harvesting fields of wheat along the way. One of the crew had a death in his family, and I'd driven a truck hauling wheat from the field to a local grain elevator. We had just crossed into Oklahoma when the crewman returned, freeing me to hit the road again.

Being flush didn't mean I was ready to spring for public transportation. Hitchhiking was my mode of travel. The last ride I'd caught dropped me off at Beegum, a town of 6,000 according to the sign at the city limits.

It was suppertime and I was hungry. I walked down the first street I came to, hoping it would intersect a main avenue with restaurants. A man sat on the sidewalk in the shadow of a vacant building next to a tavern. He slumped against the wooden structure, legs sprawled across the concrete walk.

I veered around his feet, took a couple of steps and abruptly halted. You know, the way you might if you saw a ghost from the past. Something about him stirred my memory. I stared into unfocused eyes that closed when he lifted a brown paper sack to his mouth. I knew that patrician nose and lean jaw camouflaged by his unshaven, dirt-grimed face. Halburt Duckworth had always been a handsome man. If he were cleaned up, in a suit, he'd look like Arturo Toscanini.

"Pa?"

I hadn't seen him for almost sixteen years. A frequent overnight guest at the town jail, he'd had recurring trouble with booze. But on his good days he took me fishing with him. We'd sit in the shade, lines hanging in the water, and he'd tell stories about the war. He'd been a 19-year-old sergeant, commanded a rifle squad in Viet Nam. Purple Heart. He showed me the puckered wounds on his chest where he'd been hit with small-arms fire.

One day, when I was nine, he disappeared. Vanished from our lives. I never got over the hurt of being abandoned. I knew he fought demons that I could never understand, still, how could he just walk away from us, from me, like that? Over the years I'd gone from hate to longing and back again. Now I realized I hadn't given him so much as a thought for many months.

"Pa, it's me, Custis." I kneeled beside him. He grasped the sack closer to his chest as if to protect it. "Pa, it's Custis, your son."

His eyes focused briefly, recognition showing. "Custis? You're all growed up, boy," he croaked.

He stank. His filthy clothes smelled of vomit, sweat and stale booze. I got him to his feet, his arm around my shoulder. We stumbled back to the highway where I rented a room in the Blue Moon motel, $29.95 a night, double occupancy. I stripped him and put him in the shower, laid out my razor and comb for him. "I'll be back in a few minutes," I told him. "Don't leave that shower."

I hurried uptown, found a Dollar General store and bought socks, underwear, a shirt and jeans. On the way back I picked up two bags of fast food from a Burger King. He was still under the shower, singing Yellow Rose of Texas, when I returned forty minutes later.

"Can't remember the last time I had a shower like that," he said, voice clear, sounding refreshed. I unwrapped clothes, handed them to him and watched him dress. He nodded at the fast-food bag. "That sure smells good." He sat in a chair and began wolfing down burgers, fries and coffee.

I wrinkled my nose at the heap of dirty garments on the floor. "If there's anything in those clothes you want, get it now so I can get rid of them." With his back toward me he rummaged through them and transferred items to pockets of his new clothing. I carried the pile at arm's length to the dumpster. The bottle in the brown bag went with them.

Where do you begin when you want to restore a relationship raveled by sixteen years of separation? I had no idea. I sat across from him and stared, searching for a connection, a bridge, something. He obviously had led a vagabond existence for some time. So had I. Maybe that was enough to build on—two drifters, father and son, more alike than I wanted to admit.

"Why did you do it, Pa?" I hadn't intended to begin like that, accusing him. It just came out that way. "Why did you leave us?"

He crammed fries into his mouth, licked the salt off his fingers, shook his head. "Why does anybody do anything? There's no answer, boy. People do what they do because it seems like the best thing at the time." He wagged a forefinger at me. "My advice is forget about it. People go crazy trying to figure that stuff out."

Forget about it? Not likely. "Pa, you didn't even say goodbye, just left Ma and me stranded like catfish on a mud-bank. I'll bet you don't even know she died four years ago."

He flinched like I'd slapped him. His chin dropped to his chest. I thought he might cry, but he didn't. "I didn't know," he mumbled. "I didn't know. I was afraid to ask about her." Then he did cry. Silent tears wet his newly shaven face. After a while he wiped his cheeks with a paper napkin. He had the grace to say, "I'm sorry."

I felt drained, could no longer identify my feelings

about this man. He began to speak about my mother. He talked for a long time about their good times together, how much he'd loved her, before lapsing into silence.

Finally he yawned and stretched. "I need to hit the sack, boy." He pulled the covers down on one bed, undressed and slid between the sheets. The next minute he was snoring to wake the dead. It probably had been awhile since he slept in a real bed or ate a real meal.

I watched television for a couple of hours before going to bed. I looked forward to continuing our reunion in the days ahead.

When I woke up the next morning he was gone. I thought maybe he'd stepped outside for a few minutes. That's when I noticed my billfold on the lamp table. It had been in my pants pocket. He left me with two twenties and took all the rest.

Maybe he went for breakfast, but then I saw he'd left something else behind. I picked it up and examined it. In a clear plastic envelope was his medal, The Military Order of the Purple Heart. He'd carried it with him all these years, the protective wrap keeping it unsullied. With reverent hands I held it under the lamp and admired it, his parting gift to me.

I hit the road again after breakfast. As I walked, my hand frequently returned to my shirt pocket, feeling the medal next to my heart. My old man — thief, bum, hero.

❋   ❋   ❋

I'd been down on my luck awhile, bumming rides from town to town, working odd jobs. I'd taken up residence for the night in a hay barn just inside the city limits of a place by the name of Anemia. If you believed the road sign it was home to 1,313 souls.

I'd come to accept the fact that a black cloud had positioned itself over my head and followed me with persistence. I mean, Lord knows I had plenty of problems of my own, but wherever I went trouble seemed to take root and thrive. I hoped now that a town with a ridiculous name like Anemia might change my fortunes. What more could go wrong for a town named Anemia?

When morning came I awoke from a restful sleep, brushed as much straw off me as possible and set out for the business district. Just a hop, skip and a jump down the road I came to an eating joint. The name in foot-high purple letters on the glass window was Barff's Café. I sincerely hoped that B-A-R-F-F was somebody's name.

The stools were filled with early coffee drinkers. The booths contained folks stuffing dripping pancakes into their faces, followed by sausages and eggs. The smell of food made my mouth water and my knees go weak. I felt starved, and being broke made me bolder than I normally would have been. I caught the attention of the big jowley hairy-armed man in a dirty white apron working the counter. "What can I do for ya, bud?" he asked.

I wasn't so bold that I wanted all these people to know I was a bum, so I circled the end of the counter. "What I'm standin' in the need of," I told him quietly, "is a meal and a job—in that order."

He chewed his toothpick in a thoughtful manner and rolled it across his tongue while he eyed me over like I was a second-hand vacuum cleaner. "Tell ya what, bud. There's a chair in the kitchen. You go sit on it 'til I

bring you a plate, and then you can wash these dishes."
I practically leaped toward that kitchen door. "Hold it,
bud," he commanded. I turned and looked back at him.
"What's your name?"

"Custis Duckworth," I replied and went into the
kitchen.

Later, when I was full of pancakes, eggs and sausage,
I was handed an apron, directed to a stainless steel sink
full of assorted crockery, and with a minimal amount
of instruction I began washing dishes. Two hours later
the big man behind the counter (he really was named
Barff, I learned) handed me a fistful of crumpled bills
and invited me to sit at the counter for a hit-the-road
cup of coffee. The bills were mostly ones, but there was
a five among them.

The morning crowd had thinned to a dozen or
so citizens. I sipped at my coffee and casually asked
Mr. Barff how the town came by its name. Silence descended in the cafe like a church service had broke out
and the preacher had said, "Let us pray." Heads raised
and turned in my direction. What? What did I say?

A substantial-looking matronly woman with pre-
maturely burgundy hair and a broken nose that could
use a re-setting job rose from a booth and advanced toward me. "You're not trying to start trouble, are you?"
she challenged.

"N-no, ma'am, I was just…"

"Because if you are, I'm just the old broad who can
hand it out," she assured me.

"N-no, ma'am. I was just…"

"Don't interrupt me, boy. I know your kind. Like to
start trouble, don't you?"

"N-no ma-am. I was just…"

"Hush-up, boy. Stop blathering." She was in my face by now, waving her muscular arms about, cheeks all blotchy red. "See, we had us a town meeting awhile back to discuss a possible name change, which only the most ignorant would oppose." She was wound-up now, giving us all what-for.

"Everybody in town voted to get rid of the name Anemia." She cast an accusing eye about the room and made a sweeping gesture with her arm to include one and all. "Do you know what these nincompoops wanted to name our town? Well do you?" She glared at me from left-hook distance.

"N-no, ma'am. I was just…"

"How many times do I have to tell you, boy? Just sit there and be quiet." She started over. "Do you know what they wanted to name it?" I just shook my head. "They wanted to name it Carbuncle. Carbuncle… can you imagine?" Her voice went high, and she began mimicking some unknown outsider, "What is the zip-code of Carbuncle? Oh, it's the same as Anemia's, thank you very much."

"Who do you think you are," a male voice challenged. "Why don't you tell what you la-di-dah types wanted to name the town?" This raw-boned hayseed gentleman looked directly at me. "They wanted to name it Pansy. Can you believe it? Pansy," he snorted.

"Who are you calling a la-di-dah type you Neanderthal," she bellowed. "And what's wrong with Pansy anyway?" red hair asked.

"If the shoe fits wear it, and I'll tell you what's wrong," the hayseed responded. "We'd be the laughingstock of the nation with a limp-wristed name like Pansy."

Things went rapidly downhill from there. People who had been sitting stood, a shoving match started, the noise level spiked. I turned to face Mr. Barff who gave me a quick sideways nod, indicating the kitchen. I threw him a quick salute and headed for the kitchen door. Before I could exit into the alley I heard the sound of crockery shattering.

See what I mean? Trouble. It always seemed to follow me. I was out of town by now, walking the right-hand shoulder, hoping for a ride. But I couldn't get these people out of mind. The citizens of Anemia had themselves a real problem, all right.

I believe I'd vote for Carbuncle.

I stood in the shade of a scrubby elm tree waiting for the ride I hoped would appear soon. I'd departed the town of Anemia that very morning. Rides had been scarce as hens' teeth, but I'd made it forty miles down the state highway to a crossroads called Wildweed where I'd eaten a late lunch at a gas and grocery emporium. A half-pint of milk and a fried apple pie is what I ate.

I still had eight dollars burning a hole in my pocket in anticipation of my next feeding. Hopefully, a job would materialize shortly before or after the meal. I sprinted from the shade when an aging pickup pulled to the shoulder and stopped.

"Where you headed?" the old-timer driving the truck yelled. He had a booming, thunderous voice, and I had no problem understanding him as I slid into the passenger seat.

Loose Ends

"The next town," I replied.

"Ha-ha-ha-ha," he laughed, almost loud enough to shatter glass. "You ain't choosy, are ya?" he observed in double-digit decibels. "Tell ya what," he went on, "I'm turning off up the road a piece, and I'll be going right through the biggest town here-about... near 3000 population. How does that sound to ya?"

It sounded fine. On the sly I had wadded a piece of Kleenex into my left ear. The wad provided some relief to the hammer and anvil and stirrup and whatever other parts were contained there.

"Don't take no wooden nickels. Ha-ha-ha-ha," was his parting advice when he left me by the road sign. FISTULA, the sign read. The old man had delivered me to Fistula.

I meandered down a shady street, on the lookout for a likely eating establishment. The afternoon was far spent, and my stomach was already talking to me.

Up ahead a ways, a man rushed out of a doorway onto the sidewalk. He looked frantically, first one way and then the other, arms twitching. His eyes, wide and psychotic looking, locked on me, and I slowed my pace, ready to take flight at any further signs of derangement.

He advanced toward me. "You, sir," he addressed me, "How would you like to earn fifty-dollars in the next hour?"

I took a cautious step back at his approach, prepared for physical attack. I think he took that as a negative reply to his offer. "All right then, a hundred," he added.

"There won't be any shooting involved, will there?" I inquired.

"Oh, no, no, no. Nothing like that," he assured me.

He took hold of my arm. "I need someone to judge an art contest. Our judge is indisposed… well, he's passed-out drunk is what he is." Desperation in his voice, he pleaded with me, "Please do this for me or my gallery will be ruined, my reputation in tatters. Allow me to introduce myself," he continued. "I am Fred Wickum, co-owner with my wife, Mimi, of this establishment." I noticed the sign over his door. Gilded lettering read FRED & MIMI'S ART GALLERY. "And you are?" he inquired.

"Custis. Custis Duckworth." Well, a hundred bucks being a hundred bucks, I assured him, "I'll be glad to help you out. What is it I have to do?"

"For the next hour your name is Marcel Dubois," he confided as he led me into a small dressing room. There he threw a kind of smock around my shoulders and stuffed a black beret onto my head. "There are twelve contestants," he informed me, "none of which deserves the name artist." He took my arm and guided me out the dressing room door. "Just pick the three you like best and inform me of your choices."

That sounded easy enough. "The gallery is through this door," he said. "Oh yes," he added in afterthought, "the theme of the contest is The Reclining Nude." He opened the door, propelled me through with his hand on my back and closed it behind me.

Reclining nude? Well, I've probably seen worse.

The contestants were arranged in a semi-circle, each painter standing next to an easel that supported his or her work. I walked cautiously to the first easel.

The picture was colorful, I admit. I looked at it head-on. I leaned my body to the left, I leaned it to the right. The painting appeared to be a loose pile of flesh-colored triangles with rosy splashes of pink here and there. Most of the picture, I decided, could have been painted with a roller.

One of what I thought might be a breast seemed to be in its appropriate anatomical location. The other one, if there was another one, I failed to locate among all the triangles. But an over-sized eye stared out from under what I took to be the left arm. I glanced at the artist, a slouching young man with a dangling cigarette in his mouth whose eyes seemed to be located about right.

Next was a canvas done completely in shades of blue. The subject was of interesting proportion, if a tad overweight. Like the first contestant, this was not photographic in nature but had blurred lines that I thought were distracting.

I was glad to see the third picture had a realistic look to it. I mean, you didn't have to wonder where all the parts... Holy smokes! This reclining nude was a guy. The artist, however, was of the feminine persuasion. She wore a little I'm-smarter-than-the-rest-of-you smile and stared at me over the tops of black horn-rimmed glasses. I moved quickly along to the next easel.

I came to a decision while viewing the remaining canvases. There was not one real-looking, honest-to-goodness reclining nude in the lot... if you didn't count the male. But the hundred dollars weighed heavy on my mind, so I hurried and got the job done.

I reported my findings to Fred who handed me the three medals to be awarded first, second and third. I said, "Mr. Wickum, I'd like to have my money now just in case I have to leave in a hurry. You know, disgruntled losers."

He smiled and handed me an envelope that I tore

open immediately. My faith in human nature restored by the sight and feel of two fifties, I returned to the gallery to award the prizes.

Just as I feared I was forced to depart on the run, dodging art supplies as I went out the door. The painter of triangles yelled after me, "You phony. You fake. You wouldn't know a piece of art if it were…" I slammed the door shut and exited to the sidewalk. He probably didn't understand about realism in painting. He might have been ticked-off because the girl with the guy painting was awarded a medal. Nobody likes to lose, not even non-artists.

✽　✽　✽

I'm in eastern Oklahoma after hitchhiking across most of the state. I've stayed off the interstate, traveled the two-lane highways. Elm trees have given way to oaks and occasional pines, gently rolling land to steeper hills. Pretty country.

I become aware of an unfamiliar odor on the breeze. Around a bend I come to a wooded pasture populated with goats. A frame house and outbuildings are fenced against goat invasion. Kids leap onto low-roofed sheds, butt heads with a playmate and leap back to earth. Adult goats stand on their hind legs and browse tree leaves. All this activity is accompanied by constant bleating. A hand-painted wooden sign by the driveway reads: GERALDINE & AGNES GOAT DAIRY.

I step up my pace and hurry to leave the offending smell behind. Neither am I anxious to meet up with Geraldine and Agnes. Less than 200 yards down the road a man and woman walk. They appear to be arguing, a lot of hand motion, frequent turning toward the other, raised voices.

The goat smell, less intense now, remains in the atmosphere. When I overtake the couple the man greets me with a half-hearted, "How ya doin'?"

Both he and the woman are over-dressed to be afoot in the wilderness. He wears a rumpled charcoal suit and a white shirt with no tie. She has on a black party dress. Attractive lady except that she's used too much bleach on her hair. Gives her that appliance-white look. She walks barefoot, carries a pair of black high-heels in her hand. From their appearance they could be going home after a large evening.

"Howdy," I respond and then ask, "Did your car break down?"

The woman gives me an "I wish" smile, laughs bitterly and says, "No, Daddy Warbucks here blew all our money in Las Vegas." The man didn't say anything, just walked ahead while I listened to the woman.

"Can you believe it," she says, "We won over $300,000 in a lottery, bought one-way tickets to Vegas. We planned to buy a car and drive home. While I'm playing quarter slot machines Mister Financial Genius joins the high rollers at the crap table. In less than two hours he was cleaned out. If I hadn't hit a $200 jackpot we wouldn't have had money to get out of town. As it was we barely had bus fare to Checotah."

Her husband turned and faced her. "Louise, you have a big mouth. You know that? A big mouth." His red face suggested he might be angry.

I've never been one to hang around domestic disputes very long. I stepped up my pace and left the two of them to work out their differences.

Not more than ten minutes later a pickup stopped. The lady driver leaned over, opened the passenger door and said, "Hop in, sonny."

Sonny? She couldn't have been five years older than me. Maybe ten. "I'll give you a lift into town," she offered.

"'Preciate 'ya, maam," I replied. What was that odor surrounding her? There was an aura about her that... Then it came to me. "You're not Geraldine, are you?" I inquired.

She swiveled her head to face me. "How in the world did you know that?"

"Just guessing," I told her. I thought it might not be polite to mention the eau de Toggenburg she wore.

I looked out the window and breathed through my mouth until we came to the edge of town. "Just let me out along here anywhere."

❊ ❊ ❊

It's a long way across Oklahoma. I wasn't going anyplace in particular — just going *someplace*. The morning was warming, the cobalt windless sky promised heat later. I walked in the welcome shade of elm trees lining the highway. Hitchhiking had been unproductive on this little-traveled route.

I was overtaking a man, still a quarter-mile ahead. A small dog trotted beside him. As I drew closer I could hear the man singing. "Oh, the old hen cackled from the house to the branch. The old sow whistled and the little pigs danced." His voice was strong, if not operatic.

The distance between us closed and I saw the dog was on a rope leash. But it wasn't a dog. It was a pig.

Red and black mottled, the pig had floppy ears that covered its eyes. When it wanted to observe its surroundings it lifted its head high and peered from under the offending flaps. Apparently its sense of smell was unimpaired. It detoured into the roadside grass, stuck its snout into a white fast-food bag and snacked on a few greasy French-fries. Then it chewed a catsup pouch, finally dropping the emptied plastic to the ground. French-fries always go better with catsup.

The man noticed my approach. "Howdy, neighbor." He was solidly built, maybe in his early twenties. Flaming red hair tufted from beneath a straw hat. His round freckled face, blob of a nose and wide mouth gave him the appearance of a stand-up comic.

"Nice looking pig," I said. Actually, I thought, as pigs go this one looked like he'd been short-changed at birth. The pig raised its head and peered at me from the shadows. I hoped it wasn't a mind reader. "What's its name?"

He gave me a childish grin. "I call him Snuffy on account of he's always snuffing at things." Made sense when you thought about it.

"My name's Custis," I offered.

"Glad to meet you, Mr. Custis." He resumed walking, and I fell into step beside him.

"My first name is Custis," I explained. "You don't have to call me mister."

Another grin. "My name's Lisle, but folks call me Red on account of my hair. He raised his hat so I wouldn't miss the reference. Again, it made perfect sense.

"Where did you get the pig, Red?"

He gave me a sly sideways look. "He was a gift." Right away I sensed that Red might not have the pink slip for this animal.

The leash went tight, and Red looked back. I turned with him. Snuffy was urinating. When he finished he resumed trotting. His mother must have taught him manners.

I resumed my questioning. "Who gave him to you?"

Instead of answering he said, "You wanna hear a funny song?" Before I could reply he began. "I'm nobody's moo-cow now. The bulls don't react somehow. Fuzzy lips... sunken hips... my tail's too short, and I'm minus a quart." Big grin. "Ain't that funny? There's more to it if you wanna hear it."

Ye gods. Where did he get this stuff? "That's nice, Red. Maybe some other time." He obviously wanted to keep Snuffy's origin from public knowledge.

He launched into "Sweet Betsy From Pike" and sang more verses than I would have guessed existed. It went on like that for a mile or so. "Mabel, Mabel, sweet and able, get your butt up off the table. You know darned well that two-bucks is for beer." Then "Ta-rah-rah-boom-de-ay, why don't my rooster lay? 'Cause he's not made that way, I don't care what you say." On and on.

A farm truck with a bad muffler roared past followed in short order by two sedans. None of them slowed let alone stopped to offer a ride. They may have been put off by two men accompanied by a pig. Or maybe it was the other way around.

"Toreador-ah, don't spit on the floor-ah. Use the cuspidor-ah, that's what its for-ah." Mercy. At least he seemed to be enjoying himself. Snuffy seemed stoic about it all.

I heard a car approaching from the rear. It slowed and pulled onto the shoulder ahead of us. Uh-oh. Light bar. Plunkett County Sheriff's Department. A rumpled, jowly man dismounted and tugged his pistol-belt up over his gut. Purple shades the size of china saucers hid much of his face. A second man, leathery and lean like a dustbowl farmer, emerged from the passenger side. "That there's my pig, alright," he said to the deputy.

The lawman faced me. I couldn't see his eyes. "You got any identification on you?"

I handed him my out-of-state drivers license. "Custis Duckworth." He made it sound like something you might step in. "You ain't from around here, are you, boy?" He was quick, no doubt about it.

"No, sir."

"Where 'bouts you headed, boy?" He handed back my license.

"Nowhere in particular," I answered. "Just passing through."

He got up in my face. "What do you know about this here pig?"

"Well, his name's Snuffy. That's about it." I wasn't going to lie down and roll over for him.

"Don't get smart with me, boy. We don't take kindly to thieves around here." I could feel him glowering behind the shades.

"I don't know anything about any theft," I told him. "I just happened to meet up with Red and the pig on the road." He backed off a bit.

"We'll see about that." He moved in front of Red. "What's your name, boy?"

"My name's Lisle, but folks call me Red on account of my hair." He lifted his hat for the deputy's edification.

"Boy, you in a whole lot of trouble. Now who stole the pig?" Red admitted taking the pig, and he verified my story.

The deputy returned his attention to me. "You can go now, boy. If I was you I wouldn't waste a lot of time leavin' Plunkett County." He put Red into the back seat of the cruiser. The farmer, who had taken possession of Snuffy, got into the front passenger seat, the pig on his lap. The deputy slipped behind the wheel.

Red grinned at me through the rear window, as the car made a u-turn and headed back the way it had come. I heard him singing, "Oh, she jumped in the bed and she covered up her head and she swore I could not find her... ."

I'm going to miss Snuffy.

Some of us are eccentric. Our orbital paths wobble. Mine had wobbled, hitchhiked actually, across Texas, up into Kansas and back through Oklahoma. I'd used up May through September in my wanderings, and here it was mid-October. The nights were getting cooler. I needed a place to hunker down for the winter.

The compass in my head pulled me toward home. Well, I really didn't have a home, but I realized that I was heading back to where I started my adventure. By the time I'd crossed into Arkansas and was halfway to the Mississippi I had the bit in my teeth, headed for the barn.

I'd shared a forty-mile ride in a pickup cab with an overly talkative guy and his overly friendly terrier. Every time I let my guard down the dog tried to lick my face. I stood beside the highway and watched the perky-eared mutt looking at me through the back window as the pickup receded in the distance.

Four or five rides later I walked down the lane toward my mobile home. At least it had once been mine before Phyllis decided to go her own way due to my failure to mature at a fast enough rate to suit her. "You're still a little boy," were her parting words before separating me from my car and trailer. She had me dead to rights.

The place looked well kept, not trashy like some trailers in the area. Phyllis always was neat.

I approached the door. Did she have another man? Was I just kidding myself, hoping for reconciliation? I guessed I'd soon find out. I knocked, hoping the first face I saw didn't have a beard.

The door opened. No whiskers, but it wasn't Phyllis. "Hi, Ned," I greeted my ex-father-in-law. He was about my height but heavier. Usually had a twinkle in his eye. We had always got along real well, Ned and me.

His face brightened in recognition then it immediately clouded over again. "Well look who's here," he observed with a heavy dose of sarcasm. "Are you lost or just passing through?" He backed away from the door and extended his arm in invitation. "As long as you're here you might as well come in."

I stepped into the living area and took a seat in my favorite recliner, the one facing the television set. Lord, I sure had missed that chair. "Just make yourself to home," Ned offered, again with sarcasm. He'd probably been sitting in the recliner before I knocked.

"Is Phyllis here?" I asked him.

Ned took a seat across from me. "No, she's not here, Cus. Her mother took her to the doctor."

"She's not hurt, is she?" I'd never known her to be sick a day in her life.

Ned leaned his elbows on his knees. "She's not hurt,

Cus, she's pregnant."

Well that was something of a surprise. "How did that happen?" I inquired.

Ned rolled his eyes, shook his head as in sorrow. "How dumb can one human being be?" he asked. "It happened the way most pregnancies happen. Didn't anybody ever explain to you about that?"

Still in a bit of shock, I asked, "Yeah, but who was it?"

Ned gave me that bull-at-a-bastard-calf look. "There's about four-billion people in the world, Cus, take a guess, pick one."

"Who, me?" I jabbed a finger into my chest just to be sure he got my drift.

"Give the man a cigar." He just couldn't drop the sarcasm.

The sound of a car pulling up in the driveway interrupted our conversation. "Is that them?" I rose to my feet, suddenly very nervous about the situation. Pregnant? That means... that means I'm going to be a daddy. Lord, have mercy.

Phyllis followed by her mother stepped into the room, looked at her father, looked at me. "Cus," she yelled, face beaming. Then she turned it off, just like Ned had. "Cus, where have you been?" Like she had been waiting up nights wondering why I left.

"You've gained some weight, Phil," I remarked without thinking it through first.

"No kidding." She had the sarcasm thing down pat, just like Ned, but now she was showing fight. "Are you saying I'm fat and ugly?"

What is it with women? They want you to notice their hair, a different dress, new shoes, but mention weight gain and they go off like a Roman candle. "No, Phil, I'm not saying that. It's just that you look some different."

She got in my face. "Different how?"

It came to me that I might have just one more chance to avoid a repeat eviction. "Phil," I said as gentle as I could. "Phil, you look like the Mona Lisa. You look motherly, at peace."

It must have worked. She rushed into my arms, tears sparkling. "Oh, Cus, I'm so glad you're home. Our baby needs a father, Cus. We both need you. I don't want us to ever split up again."

So that's how a week later we happened to be standing in front of the same preacher who married us the first time. It came my turn to say, "I do," and I said it loud. I knew it meant permanent retirement from hitchhiking but I'd probably get used to it. Some day I might even be able to share my adventures with my son.

Herd Animals

Zebra, shaggy wildebeest countless in their number,
untold thousands in miles-long loose formation
alternately graze then press forward in timeless cadence.
Which one leads? To whose direction do the beasts respond?
Through change of vanguard the Call remains constant.
Dumbly unaware of shifting leadership, the rearguard
follows.

Random birthing, feeding, rutting within its ranks
deters for not an instant progress of the herd.

Predators, in symbiotic brotherhood, flank the living mass.
Hyena, pride of lion, wild dog follow in hungry company.
Suffocating jaws clamp struggling throat, its bleat stifled.
The pride feeds, even as dark hooves kick in feeble protest.
Injured, old or unlucky, the prey falls in isolated terror.
The herd closes, with scarce a ripple, to heal the empty place.

With no remorse or grief, the deadly sport is played.
One life, or ten, is insignificant in the numbers game.

Human beings, intent on wealth or hedonistic pleasure,

group in vast assembly in pursuit of ease or sensual
stimulation.
In mindless precision, march; in obedience follow the flock.
Dictated chameleon goals lure the lusting, grasping
pilgrimage.
All move in common purpose to possess the trinket of
the moment,
caring not who ordains the need or what fearful price
is paid.

Random birthing, feeding, rutting, within its ranks,
deters, for not an instant, progress of the herd.

Selves, not fang or claw, menace the naive, the rash,
the weary.
Fierce competition rages for a place of fleeting notice.
Wary and covetous eyes calculate advantage over
neighbor.
Out-maneuver; contest a step; if need be, trample
underfoot.
Mankind, its own worst predator, savage in
territorial dispute,
fell many of its species unnoticed, and the trek
continues.

With no remorse or grief, the deadly sport is played.
One life, or ten, is insignificant in the numbers game.

Forbidden Fruit

"**H**urry up and shoot, Pritch." I swear that boy takes longer to make a pool shot than anybody I know. He's the same way about golf. Stands over a putt 'til you want to belt him with a three wood. He finally misses his shot and it's my turn at the table. Me and Pritch are relaxing at Bogarde's Roadhouse Cafe on a Saturday night, something we're apt to do on a semi-regular basis.

Pritch he takes a sip of brew and kind of moseys over to the window because he knows I want plenty of room when I shoot. I'm just getting lined-up when he says, "Come over here, Chauncy. You ain't going to believe this."

Pritch he's apt to get excited over the least little thing, so I say, "What is it I ain't going to believe?" and I take another sight on the nine ball.

"Get... over... here," he says with some urgency. "I'm telling you, you're not going to believe what's going on out in the parking lot." I know he won't give me any rest until I go over there, so I lay my cue on the table and join him at the window.

He is right. I can't hardly believe my own eyes.

Right out there in full view of the Almighty, Brother Buttrick's wife is dancing in the moonlight. It reminds me of that scene in Picnic where William Holden and Kim Novak slow-dance under the stars, only she's by herself. Her car door is open and I guess her radio is on. She's holding an uncapped pint bottle in one hand and the other hand is behind her head. She is swaying her hips side-to-side, and everything that's not tied down is swaying with them. She is birth naked.

Pritch he says, "That is one fine looking lady, and she needs help. I believe I am just the buck to give it to her." He puts his cue back in the rack, but I grab him before he can go outside and cause more trouble than we can handle.

"Go slow here, Pritch," I advise him.

"What do you mean, go slow? I'm already in high gear. The green flag has done dropped."

"It might not be a good thing to do, Pritch, her being a preacher's wife and all." I'm hanging onto his arm, and he's trying to pull loose. I get him turned around and we both take another long look out the window. Pritch is right again. She is sure enough one fine looking woman.

Pritch has got both hands on the windowsill now, staring hard at the parking lot. "I've seen preachers' wives before, and I'm telling you, Chauncy, she don't look nothing like no preacher's wife I ever saw. What makes you think she's a preacher's wife?" Pritch always was a stickler for details.

"Because I know her, that's how."

Me and Martin Luthur King both have us a dream. His is likely to materialize before mine. My own little dream starts a couple of weeks ago when the Buttricks move into town. I stop by the Piggly Wiggly to replenish my supply of chewing tobacco. Trophy's two-for-one package deal appeals to my frugal nature. When I walk out to my truck this perfect stranger is juggling three bags of groceries in her arms, trying to unlock her car door.

"Can I help you with that, ma'am?" I offer. I'm wishing I was wearing a hat so I could tip it.

"Why thank you," she says, big smile and bright eyes showing above a celery stalk and a bunch of bananas. I take two bags from her while she opens the door and puts the groceries inside. She's wearing a bright blue jogging suit that assumes a pleasing snugness over her more prominent features. She holds out her hand and says, "Thank you again, Mister…?

"Ballew," I tell her, shaking her hand. "Chauncy Ballew." She keeps her hand in mine longer than politeness might require, but I don't mind one bit.

"Nice to meet you, Chauncy. I'm Flossie Buttrick." She's pouring on that big smile, and I'm getting a warm sensation all over. "My husband Thurston is the new preacher at Grace Church. Are you a member?"

"No, ma'am, I'm not," I confess. I've never been churchy, but I'm already starting to re-think that.

"Call me Flossie," she says. "We'd love to see you at Sunday service, Chauncy." She gets all her parts in the driver's seat behind the wheel and leaves. I watch her car out of sight thinking there might go a shortcut to heaven.

I'm a single man. Never been married. Now Pritch

Loose Ends

he tried matrimony once. He found it too structured and confining to suit his needs. I've never had trouble finding female companionship. If a man's not too particular, there's plenty of accommodating women around. But I've made it a point not to get tangled-up with somebody else's wife. Another man's bed is a likely place to get killed.

Thinking about Flossie, my scruples begin to fade like ground fog in morning sun. This woman has class, Grade A, USDA approved. There is just no controlling the dream that forms—having her for my own. My brain knows it's only a dream, not likely to be realized, but the rest of me is not listening. The very next Sunday morning I am occupying a pew in Grace Church.

Brother Thurston Buttrick is bookish in appearance. He looks like a guy who would try living in the wilderness on locusts and honey, but he'd be wearing a good suit. He's a little on the slim side and pale. He speaks with a refined voice, but I quit watching him as soon as I spot Flossie.

She's in the choir loft, and she does about as much for a wine-colored robe as any human could. It doesn't take long for our eyes to meet. She smiles, and the flame is rekindled. I'm wondering if the choir can use an off-key baritone with a repertoire of off-color ballads. The next time I see her is the following Saturday night in Bogarde's parking lot.

Me and Pritch ease ourselves outside so as not to attract the attention of any of the bar clientele. Flossie is still going strong. She tilts the pint up, letting good whiskey dribble off her chin and disappear in a crevice below. She doesn't lose time with the music which sounds like a samba to me. She takes notice of us twenty feet away. It doesn't faze her one little bit. She takes another hit from the bottle, turns full front and slurs, "Why do'sha join the party, Chaush... Chaunshy?" She giggles and goes on with her dancing.

I step up close to her and say, "Why don't you get dressed, Flossie, and I'll take you home." Pritch is circling while she dances, keeping an eye on things.

She clasps her hands behind my neck. "Would you do that for me, Chaunsh? Help me get dressed and take me home?" I am nothing if not helpful. I take the bottle from her hand and fling it into the weeds along the edge of the lot.

Well, the three of us manage to get her into her clothes, most of them, and into her car. I toss my keys to Pritch. "Why don't you follow us in my truck?"

"How come I have to drive your truck?" he whines. Pritch can be almost childish at times.

"Just drive the damned truck, Pritch." I get into Flossie's car and shut the door.

We pull up in front of the parsonage, and I wonder how this is all going to play out. I open her door and help her to her feet about the time Brother Buttrick steps onto the front porch. Flossie runs to him and throws her arms around his neck. He must smell the whiskey, because he jerks his head to the side. "Oh, Thurston," she sobs. "These horrible men... they made me drink liquor, and they mauled me, and it was awful, just awful."

"That's a damned lie," Pritch says. He always was plainspoken. I put a hand on his arm to restrain him.

Thurston is showing outrage, face blanched, ears

red. "They didn't... they didn't... hurt you, did they, Flossie?"

She's weeping, going for an Oscar nomination. "No, Thurston, I fought them off."

Thurston might not be an NFL draft pick, but he has sand, I'll give him that. He pushes away from her and comes after me, both fists flailing. I hold him off with one hand until Pritch diverts his attention.

I'm ashamed to have to say this about Pritch, but he often lacks self-control. He delivers a kick the result of which has Brother Buttrick walking in a stooped position for the foreseeable future. I take Pritch's arm and pull him toward the truck. Flossie is consoling her husband in his time of pain. When I glance back, she smiles and mouths, "Thank you." I'm not sure if she means for the kick or for giving her a ride home.

By the time we're on the road, Pritch's adrenalin has subsided. "You missed your calling, Chauncy, you know that? You should have been a marriage counselor." Maybe.

I feel free now that I've let go of the dream. I decide to chalk it up to religious fervor. "What say we go finish our pool game, Pritch?"

Dance

The Stine Road Barn is packed, the dirt parking lot filled with pickups and cars past their prime. Bob Wills and his Texas Playboys are the attraction, a one-night stand in their tour of Valley dance halls. Don Earl leads his date, Jolene, to the entrance and pays the $4.50 admission for two. A woman sitting at a card table stamps the back of their hands with florescent ink. No drinking is allowed inside, but a steady trickle of customers exit to the parking lot to bolster festive moods from bottles secreted in their cars.

Don Earl has taken special pains with his appearance for this occasion. New stiff Levi's worn shotgun over highly polished Justin boots set off a pale green Western shirt with gold piping and mother-of-pearl snaps. His hair is slicked back with Wildroot, and he feels positively elegant. A generous application of Old Spice announces his approach from a fair distance.

The dancing crowd jostles to the lively strains of "Take Me Back To Tulsa." Vibrating guitar chords, lilting fiddles and a driven piano pace the perspiring couples. Don Earl and Jolene merge into the frenzied humanity, forced into an intimacy that ignites Don Earl's fantasies.

He's invested in a lot of unneeded coffee and peach pie at the Circle Dot café where Jolene is a counter waitress. For two weeks he's stolen time from his job at the welding shop across the highway from the café. Hesitant and unsure of himself, he conducts a low-intensity unilateral courtship. When she agrees to go dancing he isn't sure if she smiles from pleasure or if she is laughing at him.

The band is playing "The Keeper Of My Heart." The slower tempo and Jolene's softness are the stuff hasty marriages are made of. Don Earl whispers in her ear a line inspired by a remembered movie, "Be mine, Jolene, be mine." With his cheek pressed against her hair Don Earl doesn't see her lifted brows and rolled-up eyes.

About the time the trumpet solo kicks-in on "Time Changes Everything" Don Earl feels a firm hand tapping his shoulder. "How 'bout I cut in, podner?"

Don Earl turns and looks up into the face of a raw-boned sun-burnt grinning field-hand.

"Jolene, darlin'," the redneck says, familiar as sweat, "How 'bout me an you dancin' a spell?" Jolene obviously knows him. Her face lights up in a broad smile and she slips gracefully into the interloper's arms.

Well, nothing in recent memory has hurt Don Earl like this has. He is an island among dancing couples, dejected and alone, Jolene lost among the dimly lit bodies. He works his way out the door, fighting back tears. At his car he fishes the pint bottle from under the front seat, slides in under the wheel and takes a long pull of the fiery fluid. After the second and third drink his courage is in revival. He considers a physical attack on the field-hand, in his clouded mental state overlooking the obvious disparity in size. This guy is big enough to break Don Earl in half.

Then he sees Jolene and the big guy walk to a Chevy truck three down from his car. Don Earl drunkenly opens his door and gets out, but by this time the pickup is headed out of the lot. He watches the taillights pull onto Stine Road and disappear into the night. He tilts and drains the bottle, flings it into the dark and pounds his hand on the car.

"Damn," he cries. "Four dollars and fifty cents right down the drain."

Hazel

Six o'clock in the morning and I walked stretching and yawning into the bunkhouse dining room. During the summer breakfast was at five. We changed the clocks for Daylight Savings Time but not our routine. Shorty sat at the table, a mug of coffee and the San Francisco Examiner in front of him. An early riser, Shorty drove a half-mile down to the highway every morning to get the paper, which he read like a man possessed.

I continued past him to the kitchen. "Morning, Hazel. What's for breakfast?" Skillets heated on the gas range, a black iron structure the size of a young war ship. A bowl of brown eggs sat among the various containers cluttering the flour-dusted countertop. The smell of biscuits rose from the oven. I grabbed a clean cup and filled it from the urn.

Hazel chuckled, a series of deep, good-natured alto notes. "You know what's for breakfast. The same thing you people want for breakfast every morning." She began laying thick slices of ham in the skillet. "Get on out of here and don't bother me."

I carried my coffee out and took a chair across from Shorty. The table was long enough to seat twelve, but we always gathered at the end closest to the kitchen. "What's going on in the world?" He glanced at me and handed me the green sheets before I could ask for them. The sports world was slow in winter months, but I liked to keep up with baseball rumors.

"Well," he began. He'd begin a running commentary on world events while I looked for news about DiMaggio or Schoendienst. "Jews are killing Arabs and Arabs are killing Jews." He always reported in a so-what voice no matter what degree of calamity was afoot. The Russians could land at Fisherman's Wharf and not merit a raised eyebrow from Shorty. "They're bombing busses and buildings in Haifa. The UN split that little Podunk country last year, and the blood hasn't stopped running since."

Apparently satisfied he'd given adequate coverage to the Mid-east he jumped to Asia. "Some guy assassinated Mahatma Gandhi. Steps out of a crowd and plugs him with a pistol." Mears had come in during the news roundup and taken a seat next to Shorty.

"Who is this My-hat feller?" Mears had been shortchanged at birth, maybe some wires left unconnected in his brain. It didn't seem to dampen his interest in the world around him. He probed from several directions every fact that came his way, then immediately forgot what he'd learned.

"He's a Indian," Shorty said from behind his paper. Over time, Shorty had developed endless patience with Mears. Mears was quick to test it.

He studied his coffee, scratched at his receding hairline. "I thought Indians all had names like Bull Run or Geronymous. What you said don't really sound like no Indian to me." Shorty laid the paper aside in prepara-

Loose Ends

tion for a tedious session about Asian Indians versus the American variety. Hazel saved the day for him. She set a platter of hot fried ham and a bowl of scrambled eggs on the table. Mears forgot about Indians and focused on eggs. "They ain't no bad eggs in scrambled eggs," he declared. He said the same thing every morning.

By the time we were getting our elbows unlimbered, Hazel was back with a platter of biscuits and a bowl of sausage gravy. Conversation came to a stop for a frantic ten minutes of eating. I guess nobody in the world could make biscuits as good as Hazel's.

When Mears finished his plate, he said what he said every morning when he finished his plate. "Hazel, you are a pearl without no pride." He must have heard some preacher read from the Bible about pearls without price. It stuck with him, but he had it garbled some. Anyway, it made Hazel smile, and it did have a poetic ring to it.

When the last smear of gravy had been wiped clean with the last biscuit, Shorty scooted his chair back. He was foreman of Rancho Tres Robles and made the daily duty assignments after breakfast. "Mears, why don't you tinker with that Ford tractor and see if you can get it running. I'll ride with Gaines up to the feed barn and check with you when I get back." Mears might be lacking in some of his compartments, but he was on the same wavelength with any contraption with moving parts and a purpose.

Shorty and me left the warmth of the bunkhouse and climbed into the Jeep, headed for the hill pasture to feed cows. Feeding was my job, but when there wasn't a lot of work to do sometimes he'd go along. He drove the Jeep.

He smoked roll-your-own cigarettes, one dangling from his mouth now. Every so often he'd remove the cigarette from his lips and spit out a shred of tobacco. The lower windshield and dashboard were peppered with dried and drying remnants of his habit.

A gimpy left leg, the result of a Japanese mortar fragment on Okinawa three years previous, gave him a rolling, seafarer's gait. He'd seen two years of Marine Corps action in the Pacific theater. I could sit for hours listening to his war stories.

World War II was winding down by the time I was old enough to enlist. I guess I'd always carry some guilt feelings about that. I used to imagine myself with beribboned chest, saluting smartly and saying, "Pvt. Gaines Woodard reporting for duty, Sir!" Now, in 1948, that boyhood dream had faded, all but died out. I still hadn't found one to replace it. I was content with my world on the ranch with people I liked. There was nothing beyond the horizon calling to me.

The Jeep bumped over the last rise, and Shorty brought us to a stop near the feeding barn. The tin-roofed building was open to the weather on two sides. The hayloft above stored the winter supply of baled hay.

Shorty didn't like climbing the ladder into the loft. "I'll spread the cake," he said, "if you'll get the hay." We carried an eighty-pound sack of cottonseed cake in the back of the truck. These were mamma cows, due to start calving in a couple of months, and they needed a daily protein boost.

I clambered up the creaky ladder. A sweet-musty blend of grass hay and mouse odor hovered in the cold air. Hay, stacked to the rafters, filled two-thirds of the space. I began dragging bales, one at a time, into position above the manger until I had formed a broken line the length of the loft. Forty-two white-faced cows looked up at me while they jostled each other, sorting out their pecking order. I went down the line of bales, pulling off baling wire and kicking the hay into the manger until all the animals were feeding.

I'd just kicked the last bale over the side when my eye caught movement. It didn't worry me much, because I'd seen a feral cat around the barn at different times. A big gray-striped female, she enjoyed a bountiful supply of mice when the loft was full. Thinking she may have attracted an itinerate tom and had a litter of kittens, I walked back along the haystack, peering into the occasional gaps.

Several bales had been shifted, I could tell, leaving a sizeable hole in the bottom row. I hunkered down to investigate. There staring back at me was a scruffy-looking, shivering kid. He'd built himself a hay igloo long enough for him to stretch out but not high enough to sit up. He startled me, but he didn't look like he could be dangerous to anybody past sixth-grade.

"You're going to freeze to death in there." His den was the warmest part of the barn, out of the wind, but it still must have been close to forty degrees in the loft. I'm twenty, and I guessed the kid to be about thirteen. "You'd better come out, and we'll go down to the bunk-house where it's warm and get something to eat."

That seemed to interest him, and he crawled out looking like a stray mutt. Leaves and stems clung to his baggy shirt and jeans, his stringy hair. He didn't have a coat or hat. Skinny shoulders shook in spasms. I'd bet it had been a while since he'd had a meal. I took off my flannel-lined jacket and put it on him. He still hadn't said anything.

"What's your name, kid?" No response. He just stared at his feet and shook. "Well, come on then. Let's get back to the ranch."

He climbed down the ladder behind me. Shorty was leaning against the Jeep, smoke curling up past one squinted eye. "Looks like you got yourself a stray there, Gaines."

"Found him in a nest about half froze. Maybe we'd better get him down the hill and feed him." We put the kid in the back seat and started for home. This war-surplus Jeep didn't have a heater. Even with the canvas doors closed it was plenty cold.

I looked over my shoulder into the back. "Where you from, kid?" He threw me a sideways glance but said nothing. "Somebody's probably worried about you," I suggested, but I couldn't break through the wall he'd thrown up between himself and the world.

We pulled up beside the bunkhouse. Shorty stayed behind the wheel. "I need to check on Mears," he said. "He might have that tractor climbing trees by now." I got out and motioned for the kid to follow.

A stand-up oil heater had the dining area toasty. I could hear Hazel rattling pans in the kitchen. Hazel was from Nowata, Oklahoma. How she ended up as cook on this northern California ranch was a mystery to me. She was a Godsend to the transient bunch of cow-boys and laborers who worked here during hay season and wheat harvest before drifting on. She dished out steaming helpings of beef stew or roast or meatloaf and seemed to delight in their ravenous appetites.

The only time she left the ranch was when I drove her down to Willowdale on Saturdays to do the grocery shopping. Her social life didn't suffer, though. She had a boyfriend, Charlie Feathers, who played piano in a club five nights a week. He visited almost every Monday night, Hazel entertaining him in her rooms.

I walked to the kitchen doorway. "Hazel, do you suppose you can scare up some eggs and ham for this boy?" She turned from the sink and inspected our guest. I'd never heard her say a cross word to anyone, but her dark face stiffened. She placed both hands on her plump hips and demanded, "When's the last time you washed, boy?" She gave me the benefit of her disapproving stare. "Take him into the bathroom and get him cleaned up before he puts a foot under my table. There's some old clothes in the washroom that might fit him." She turned back to the sink.

After showing him to the bathroom and giving him a change of clothes I returned to the kitchen and poured a cup of hot coffee. I told Hazel how I'd come to find the kid, and her mothering instinct kicked-in. "That poor child," she said. "That poor, poor child."

That was when we heard a vehicle pull up outside. A car door slammed, and Deputy Howdy Hurst of the Shasta County Sheriff's Department moseyed in. He regularly patrolled this area and often stopped by for coffee. "Come on back, Howdy," I called. "Coffee's hot." I poured him a cup and we sat at the table, leaving Hazel to her cooking. "Cold enough for you?" I asked to make conversation.

"I'll tell you what," he drawled. Howdy worked at being Western. His narrow-brim Stetson and stitched lizard-skin boots weren't part of his regulation uniform, but they supported his image. "I ain't been warm for about 36 hours." He took a tentative sip of coffee and cupped the crockery mug in his hands. "Some yahoo and his girlfriend tried to heist Boots Sanford's filling station down at the highway junction day before yesterday. Old Boots wasn't having no part of it and put a .38 slug into the guy's backside. The girl took off on foot, and me and half the department have been tramping over this end of the county looking for her." He blew on the steaming liquid before trying another sip.

A little shiver ran through me. I glanced at Hazel. She'd been listening, and she gave me a frown that told me to keep my mouth shut. I asked Howdy, "What does this girl look like?"

Howdy pulled a can of Prince Albert out of his shirt pocket and began rolling a cigarette. He hadn't mastered the technique yet, and he ended up with a lumpy smoke that looked like a short snake had swallowed a plump rabbit. Shreds of tobacco scattered down his shirt and on the table. I thought he was carrying this image thing too far. "We don't have a picture of her, but she's a 110 pound blonde, age seventeen. Name's Cindy Hairston. Ran off and left her purse in the car. Can you beat that?" Howdy flicked a big kitchen match with his thumbnail and set fire to the twisted end of the cigarette. The brown paper flared, and he jerked his head back to save his eyebrows.

He looked at his watch, took a big gulp of coffee that must have burned all the way down. "I've got to run," he said. "Catch you folks later. Thanks for the coffee, Hazel," and he was gone.

Hazel came over and sat beside me. "You think we did

the right thing by not mentioning the kid?" I asked her.

She nodded. "We don't know this is a girl. She looked like a boy to me."

"Yeah, but..."

"I don't want to hear no 'yeah, buts.' Even if it is the girl, I can't send her off hungry and scared." She frowned and twisted her hands. "Sometimes all a child needs to get straightened out is a little help, somebody to care."

The kid walked in. He, or she, had showered, wet hair combed back slick. The jeans and chambray shirt fit tighter than his old clothes. Hazel took one look and whispered to me, "What do you think now?"

Since she mentioned it, the kid did look a little bit too chesty and hippy for a thirteen-year-old boy. Hazel was on her like a duck on a June bug. "Sit here at this table, honey, while Hazel gets you somethin' to eat." She wheeled on me. "Get her a glass of orange juice and a cup of coffee while I whip up those eggs. Hurry up now."

Hazel set enough food in front of the girl to feed a thresher crew. She hadn't admitted she was a girl, but she hadn't denied it either. She put away a pile of scrambled eggs, ham and wheat toast with grape jelly without lifting her head. All of this with Hazel and me sitting there staring at her.

When the girl finished eating and sat back in her chair, Hazel asked, "Are you ready to talk to us now, honey? We can't help you if you don't talk to us." The girl just looked at her lap, sullen and silent. "We know your name is Cindy Hairston, honey. No need to try and hide anymore," she purred, her voice comforting and gentle as a flannel sheet.

The girl's eyes widened, startled. "How did you know?" I knew right then why she'd kept quiet all this time. I'm not so dumb I can't tell a girl's voice from a boy's. She glanced left, then right, a bird ready to take flight, but there was no place to go.

Hazel reached across the table and placed her hand on the girl's. "While you were taking a shower a deputy stopped by and told us about the holdup and who they were looking for."

She stared at Hazel's brown hand, and her lower lip trembled. Her eyes brimmed with tears. "Why are you doing this?" The tears broke and streamed down her cheeks. "Why didn't you tell the deputy about me?"

Hazel seemed to have a mother-hen mission in life. I'd seen her time and again get all broody and spread her wings over some down-and-outer with a sad story. Matter of fact, she'd done the same for me. I guess she'd been there herself—no money, no friends and no place to roost. She slid her chair back, moved around the table and sat beside the girl. She laid her arm protectively around the slim shoulders. "Cindy, honey, I couldn't stand the thought of them hauling you off to some cold jail cell. Why don't you tell Hazel about it, and maybe we can figure what to do?"

Something caught in my chest. The girl looked so forlorn and vulnerable I was tempted to put my arm around her. I might have if Hazel hadn't already staked a claim there.

"I ran away from home in Klamath Falls," she began. Her eyes were weepy and downcast, her voice a subdued murmur. Hazel found a tissue somewhere in her bosom and gave it to the girl. "My father told me Brad was no good and ordered me to stop seeing him."

Tears flowed freely again. "He was right. God, I wish I had listened to him."

Hazel looked at me and pointed to a box of tissues on the sink-board. I fetched the box and set it in front of the crying girl. Weeping women make me nervous, but there was no way I could escape without Hazel noticing.

Well, it turned out Brad decided they needed some cash about the time they reached Willowdale. When he showed her the gun, Cindy begged him not to use it. He convinced her it was just for show. She waited for him in the car, nervous and scared. When the fireworks started, she was terrified the owner would shoot her. She piled out of the car and ran into nearby woods. After walking most of the night she found the barn and did her best to make a warm place in the hay.

"I have to get home," she sobbed. "Mom and Dad will be so worried."

Hazel patted her and clucked over her. "Don't you worry none, Cindy, honey. We'll see to it you get back to your family."

As it happened, the next day was Saturday, shopping day. After I got back from feeding, the three of us squeezed into the Jeep and headed for Willowdale. Hazel had washed Cindy's clothes, came up with a cap and a Levi jacket and had her looking like a boy again. I dropped Hazel off at the Safeway where she and the girl exchanged tearful goodbyes. Then Hazel handed her $50. Unless I missed my guess, Hazel couldn't afford it. That was probably mattress money she'd been saving.

I kicked-in $5 myself, that being all that stood between me and payday. I worked on the ranch for room and board and $125 a month. It wasn't easy for me to part with the five, but I was ashamed not to.

At the Continental Trailways depot I walked inside with Cindy and stood back while she went to the counter. Two people were in line ahead of her, but I waited. I was going to make darned sure she got on that bus. She came back, ticket in hand, threw her arms around my neck and planted a kiss on my mouth. It didn't last near long enough. She drew away, her eyes looking into mine. Funny, I hadn't noticed how blue they were before. "I don't know how I'll ever be able to thank you," she said and ran for the departures door. I blushed when I saw a couple of people staring at me. Two boys kissing must have caused a little shockwave to run around the room.

When her bus backed out of its slot the destination sign on the front read SACRAMENTO, not KLAMATH FALLS. Sure enough, when it reached the corner it turned south instead of north. That lying little tramp had snookered us. I was hot under the collar, but I reached up and touched the kiss where I felt it smoldering on my lips.

When I picked-up Hazel and the groceries, I still hadn't figured how to break the news to her. "Did she get off alright?" Hazel wanted to know.

I chickened out. I looked into those dark, motherly eyes filled with concern and couldn't bring myself to tell her. "No problem," I answered. Hazel's beatific smile was enough to seal my tingling lips forever.

On the way home we met Howdy coming the other way. He flicked his lights and waved. We waved back. "Don't you never ever tell Howdy about none of this. Promise?"

"You can depend on it, Hazel."

Hazel surprised me. We'd returned from town, and

Loose Ends

I'd just finished carrying groceries into the kitchen. Cindy's parting kiss lingered in my mind. "We need to go back to town this evening," Hazel said, her back turned to me. She lifted four gallon-jugs of milk into the big refrigerator, glass clinking against glass. "Hand me that orange juice."

I gave her the jug of fresh-squeezed. "What do you mean go back? Did you forget something?"

She chuckled, still in high spirits about Cindy, thinking she'd restored an innocent child to the straight and narrow, I guess. "No, I didn't forget nothing." She closed the refrigerator door and turned to me. "Charlie's been wanting me to come hear him play at the club, and tonight's the night."

"I don't have any money, Hazel. I gave the last I had to that... uh, to Cindy."

She chuckled again. "You won't need no money. Besides, you'll get your reward in heaven." I wasn't going to hold my breath for that puny amount. If anyone got a reward worth mentioning it would be Hazel.

"I don't have any dress-up clothes," I stalled. "And besides, I'm not twenty-one. They won't let me in that place." I really wanted to listen to a Bob Hope special on the radio, but Hazel was determined.

"Just put on something clean and don't worry about it." She eyed me up and down. "You look close enough to twenty-one to me. We need to leave about seven-thirty. Now get on out of my way and let me finish-up here."

Five minutes early I fidgeted in the dining room, too nervous to sit. I was dressed in clean Levis, my good shirt, the one with pale blue and white stripes and the fake pearl snaps down the front and on the cuffs, and my good boots. I didn't own a clean hat, so I was bareheaded.

"Don't you look nice," Hazel said, cheerful as a girl with a full dance card. My eyes almost popped out. Hazel had on a slinky black dress with a red tropical flower design, hibiscus or something. A strand of big pearls gleamed above her full bosom. Man, she really looked uptown. "What do you think about Hazel's glad-rags?" She did a slow pirouette, hands fanned out at her sides, big smile.

"We're just going to Willowdale, Hazel, not New York City." Hazel was thirty-something, a little on the plump side, but she'd turn heads in that outfit. "You look like a million bucks," I finally told her. That made her smile. I haven't really figured out women yet. They give orders like they were born to command, and the next minute they're dying for a compliment. Makes you wonder.

The Starlite Club was one of those highway places your mother would advise you to stay away from. Dinner and drinks were the attraction, no dancing. Charlie Feathers provided the kind of music that kept the clientele lingering at their tables in boozy conversation.

Charlie was in the middle of "Sophisticated Lady" when we walked in. Hazel has a record collection that she plays, much of it from the thirties and early forties. I knew most Duke Ellington tunes and recognized the song right away. Charlie spotted us, called a waiter over to the piano and whispered to him. We immediately were shown to a down-front table with a reserved sign on it. I was a little self-conscious about it all. It seemed like everybody was staring at us, a wet-behind-the-ears pale cowhand type trailing along behind a spiffy dark-skinned lady. I figured it would take too long to explain the situation to everyone, so I kept my head down and tried to look suave.

Charlie finished his number, came over to our table and kissed Hazel on the cheek. He shook hands with me. Charlie is a smooth kind of guy. He's a few years older than Hazel, a little gray showing in front of his ears. He sports a mustache that's about as wide as you could make with one swipe of a dull crayon. He pomades his hair down slick and wears natty checks or plaids. "I have to get back to the piano," he said. "You folks order up, it's on the house." I think what he meant was that it was on him. Nice guy, Charlie.

He began playing "Bangles and Baubles" or "Baubles and Bangles," I forget which, with a real jazzy beat. I grinned at Hazel. "He can really make that thing talk, can't he?"

"He's the best." She giggled. "That man has a lot of talents."

"Are you going to marry him, Hazel?" I just blurted it out. I knew it was none of my business, but I hoped she wasn't thinking about giving up cooking for us.

She threw her head back in a laugh that came up from her lower regions. Charlie and people around us glanced our way. She lowered her voice. "Lord no, I'm not going to marry him. That man's been married so many times he's developed immunity. If I was to marry him he'd be gone in a heartbeat, playing piano in Memphis or Hot Springs with Hazel stuck in Willowdale." She patted my hand reassuringly. "Hazel's not going to desert you." That was good to hear, let me tell you.

The waiter brought our drinks. I'd ordered an Oly, beer being all I was used to. He'd given me a hard look but didn't ask for ID. Hazel ordered a grasshopper. I'd never heard of such a thing but didn't want to look dumb by asking what it was. She sipped her way through three of those green concoctions while I nursed my beer.

By eleven o'clock I was sleepy. Charlie's music was nice to listen to, but it was past my bedtime and the beer made me yawn. Hazel leaned over and said, "Maybe we'd better get on home." We thanked Charlie, said our goodbyes and left.

The night was chilly as we walked across the parking lot. Hazel did little dance steps while she sang and hummed "It Takes Two To Tango." About the time she said, "Darling, it always takes two," I took hold of her arm and stopped.

"There's someone in the Jeep, Hazel." Whoever it was opened the door and slid out.

"Cindy, honey," Hazel cried out. They were in each other's arms like a cow and calf that had been separated and reunited. The little sneak hadn't been gone fourteen hours, and here they were acting like she'd just returned from Outer Mongolia. But I wouldn't be honest if I didn't tell you my heart was thumping like a dog's tail on a wood porch. Hazel asked, "How did you find us, honey?"

"I was walking by and noticed the ranch name on the Jeep," she answered. "It was cold, so I waited inside." RANCHO TRES ROBLES was painted across the front under the windshield, and I'd parked close to the road. I stood there feeling dumb and wondered, hoped she would kiss me. No such luck. "Oh, Hazel, I'm so sorry about what I did," she said.

"What was it you did, honey?" Oh, oh. Here comes trouble.

"Didn't he tell you?" She was looking at me.

"Tell me what?" Hazel shot me a glance that would curdle milk. She was starting to show fight.

"I didn't buy a ticket to Klamath Falls, I bought one to Sacramento." She looked at me again and smiled. "Gaines was watching the bus. I'm sure he knew."

Hands on hips, Hazel demanded, "Why didn't you tell me that?" Hazel could be intimidating, and she was making me feel small and useless.

When in doubt, tell the truth, my mama used to say. "I just couldn't do it, Hazel. I thought it would spoil everything for you." She glared at me for a beat then tears came to her eyes before she hugged me.

"Ain't you something," she said. I struggled awhile before she turned me loose.

Cindy told us she'd changed her mind about running and decided to go home. She'd asked the driver to stop the bus she'd been on, and she'd hitchhiked back to Willowdale. "I was going back to the depot to catch a bus to Klamath Falls when I saw the Jeep." She pulled a wad of bills out of her pocket. "I still have enough for my ticket."

"You're doing the right thing, honey," Hazel told her. We crowded into the Jeep and drove to the depot.

I don't know what it is about goodbyes that kill conversation. We had a twenty-minute wait, and Hazel must have asked Cindy a half-dozen times if she needed anything. Her bus was called, and Cindy and Hazel hugged like wrestlers trying for a fall.

When it was my turn you could have knocked my hat off if I had been wearing one. She threw her arms around me and planted a kiss right here on my mouth. I hung on and prolonged it until she finally broke away and ran for the door. My knees were weak, and though my inclination was to run after her, I stood my ground. Hazel's eyes were big as biscuits. Surprised, I guess.

We hadn't no more than got in the Jeep when Hazel started in on me. "You two done that before, didn't you?"

I was trying to act like none of this bothered me, but I still had a case of the trembles. I quick-glanced Hazel. "Done what before?"

"You know what I'm talking about. That wasn't the first time you and her kissed, was it?"

Since my mama died a few years back, Hazel was the nearest thing to mother I had. If anybody else asked me what she asked I'd have told them it was none of their bees-wax, but I couldn't tell Hazel that. I couldn't help grinning. "She kissed me this morning when I put her on the bus." My face felt hot.

Hazel must have thought that was funny, because she sure had herself a good laugh. "I'll bet it's not going to be easy keeping you out of bus depots from now on." I didn't see the humor, but she laughed most of the way back to the ranch. It's hard to be mad at your foster mother.

Weekends in the bunkhouse were usually quiet this time of year. On occasion Shorty and Mears drove to town on a Saturday night for a couple of beers and to get their ashes hauled in a back-stairs madam's emporium. Being on the fuzzy-cheek side of twenty-one, I was never invited. I was too young to be welcome in either a bar or a cathouse.

Sunday night I watched Shorty and Mears at the dining room table over a checkerboard. Shorty was the better player, but Mears learned he could be distracted into making a mistake. "Reckon what could be making that engine run rough?" Shorty studied his move with no indication he'd heard Mears. "Sounds like tika-tika-pah, tika-tika-pah." He paused, serious eyes focused on Shorty who studiously ignored him. "Sometimes it's more like tik-tik-tika-pah. You ever hear it do that before?" Mears could keep this going all night. I got up and retreated to my room.

Eight feet long and eight feet wide, this was my personal space. A sash window looked out onto a roofed porch. Furnishings consisted of a single bed, a dresser and an apple box to set my radio on. A small, open closet in one corner held my scant wardrobe. Several tattered paperbacks were scattered in the apple box.

I lay on the bed, turned the radio on and waited for the tubes to warm. The Arvin radio was about the size of a half-loaf of bread and didn't receive the new FM stations. Music finally emerged, Les Brown's Band of Renown playing "Leapfrog."

My mind drifted from the bouncy music to the soft kisses I'd received yesterday. That Cindy. She must be home in Klamath Falls by now. An unfamiliar longing came over me. Did I miss her? Well, I guess that's what this hollow feeling was all about. I tried to clear my mind by studying the Varga girl pictures I'd torn out of Esquire Magazines and pinned on my wall. Blonde, leggy and busty, they all reminded me of Cindy. They did little for my peace of mind.

After a restless night, I welcomed daylight. I fed the cattle after breakfast, and when I returned to the bunkhouse Howdy's car was parked close to the door. Hazel was handing him a cup of coffee and a cinnamon roll when I walked in. I grabbed one of each for myself, and we sat at the table. If there's anything Hazel makes better than biscuits it's cinnamon rolls.

Howdy dipped the roll into his coffee and smacked his lips around the soggy bun. He talked with the wad of dough in his mouth. "You know that Hairston girl we were looking for?" He leaned over his cup and gulped another soggy mouthful of bun. I wanted to shake him. Get to it, man. What about her? "M-m-ph. We're not looking for her any more." He wiped a sleeve across his mouth. I let a lung-full of air escape. "She wasn't really involved, just along for the ride." He washed down the last of the bun with a sip of coffee. "From what Old Boots and the boyfriend told us, she didn't have anything to do with the holdup."

Hazel had tuned in and come up behind me. "That sure is good news," she crowed. "I knew that little girl was worth helping." She clapped her hand over her mouth and hurried into the kitchen.

Howdy blinked once, twice. "What did she mean by that?"

A few mornings later I was on my way to feed. There hadn't been hardly a minute since she left that Cindy wasn't on my mind. As I pulled to a stop by the barn I saw a rider coming. Even at 200 yards I could tell it was the Rocha girl from the neighboring ranch. I'd seen her once or twice when she'd been to the ranch house with her father. I didn't know her name.

She rode a kind of wild-eyed skewbald mare, red-roan and white in color. The mare slung her head around, shied

Loose Ends

at bushes and pranced sideways as she approached.

The girl rode right up to me and sat in the saddle giving me the once-over without speaking. She took her time about it. I was getting nervous, so I tipped my hat and said, "Ma'am." She had the blackest hair and whitest skin I believe I've ever seen on the same person. In the past I'd seen a couple of Portagee women with that coloring.

"Your west fence is down," she said. "A couple of cows broke through it. I ran them back in, but the fence needs fixing." She sat up on that crazy mare looking down on me. I figured that was the end of the message.

"'Preciate it, Ma'am. I'll get over there and take care of it." She was still staring at me, only now she had a little smile.

"You're kind of cute, cowboy." Well I wasn't expecting that, let me tell you. I wished I wasn't so bad to blush. She got down off the mare, still smiling. "You came here to feed?" I nodded. "I'll help you," she said, and tied the mare to a post.

Don't ever follow a woman up a ladder. It's bad for your heart. With her helping it didn't take half the time to feed the cows. She pitched right in like she'd done this kind of work before.

Just when I thought we were done I found out we were just getting started. I've never been attacked by a mountain lion, but I'd guess it'd be a lot like what happened next. She tore at my clothes and had her mouth on mine. I started out fighting her off, but somewhere along the way I changed sides and started to lend a hand.

I was worried about, you know, precautions, but there wasn't any need to. This woman was a walking drugstore. Another thing that worried me was this was my first time, and I wanted to be on the same page as her, not playing a different tune. I worried for nothing, because she was conductor, brass, wind, strings and percussion all rolled into one.

It ended as sudden as it began. She started jerking on her clothes. "I have to go. See you around, cowboy," and down the ladder she went.

I really hated to see her leave. She was such a friendly girl, and I thought we were getting along pretty good. Then it hit me. I hadn't thought about Cindy for twenty minutes. And that ache seemed to be gone. I needed to do some deep thinking about all this.

I went down the ladder a couple of minutes after the girl. She was long gone out of sight. I wished I'd thought to ask her name.

We always carried fencing tools and wire in the Jeep, so I headed right out to find and mend the break. I drove on the ranch road that follows the fence-line until I came to the gap. On the far side of the fence I could see that roan mare's rump disappear into a growth of trees. A wistful sigh escaped from somewhere. I stood there moon-eyed for a bit, and then I started mending fence.

The next Friday after the hayloft incident, I was in the dining room a few minutes before lunch gabbing with Mears. I'd just replaced a burned-out light bulb over the table. Mears sat and gazed up at the bulb. "Reckon how them light bulbs work," he mused. Even if I knew how they worked I wouldn't have attempted to explain it to him.

Luckily, about that time Shorty entered. He'd picked up the mail at the box down by the highway. "One letter for Hazel, postmarked Willowdale," he announced as he handed it to her. Probably from Charlie Feathers.

"One letter for Gaines, postmarked Klamath Falls." He held it behind him out of my reach, big grin on his face. "You don't want this, do you, Gaines?"

"Don't be teasing the boy," Hazel said with a chuckle, her eyes sparkling. Shorty handed me the letter. From Klamath Falls, sure enough. I headed for my room, tearing into the envelope as I walked.

"Dear Gaines," it began. My pulse rate spiked. "I wish I could thank you and Hazel again in person for your kindness to me." She'd written it in green ink, nice neat hand. "Enclosed are two money orders, one for Hazel and one for you to repay what you gave me." Sure enough, inside the envelope were the money orders, one for $50, the other for $5.

"I've been telling my parents about you, and they'd like to meet you. Daddy is a building contractor and can always use good help. He said that if you're half the man I say you are he'll give you a good job." I paused to catch my breath. She continued, "Please come as soon as you can." The letter was signed, "Love, Cindy."

I laid back on my bunk and read it again, slowly, while I savored the sight and sound of "Love, Cindy."

"Food's getting cold," Shorty said when I went back into the dining room. "Better hurry and catch up."

"Just a second," I told him and handed the money order to Hazel.

She read it and beamed. "That sweet child," she said, tears glistening in her eyes.

I had a lot to think about now. I hated to entertain the idea of leaving people who were like family to me. Shorty, Mears and especially Hazel I'd miss terribly. But there really was no future for me working on ranches the rest of my life. I'd seen too many bums come and go, year after year, men with no past and no future, moving from bunkhouse to bunkhouse with the seasons. I owed it to myself, I decided, to at least go visit Cindy and see what her father had to offer.

There was one other thread holding me here, that girl on the crazy mare. Somewhere in the back of my mind I'd nourished the hope that we might meet up again. Who could forget an experience like that? But that dream had waned with the passing of days. I now realized that the Portagee girl, while pleasant company, was just a tad too wild for my taste. Cindy seemed like a better long-term choice.

I kept my thinking under my hat until after supper Saturday night. Hazel made one of my favorite dishes, crab gumbo. I was full as a tick, had that well-fed feeling. I took Hazel aside and showed her Cindy's letter. Her lip trembled while she read, and tears rolled down her cheeks. "You're going to leave, aren't you?" She didn't say it accusingly, just matter-of-fact.

I nodded. I wish she wouldn't cry. It makes it all so much harder for me.

I gave two weeks notice to Shorty, and on the second Saturday after, I rode into Willowdale with Shorty driving and Hazel along to do her grocery shopping. Shorty stopped at Safeway, and I got out of the Jeep with Hazel. I felt like a little boy in her farewell embrace. I'd be lying if I told you I didn't need to wipe my eyes and blow my nose before I got back in the Jeep.

At the bus depot Shorty shook my hand and wished me well. "Look after Hazel," I told him before boarding the bus.

❊　❊　❊

　Loose Ends

I never saw Hazel again. She wrote a letter a few months after I left. She'd changed her mind and was marrying Charlie Feathers. They were moving to Los Angeles.

Cindy and I married the next year after I went to Klamath Falls. We've enjoyed a long rewarding marriage and have the added blessing of growing old together. We've been honest and true to each other over the years. Well, I've never mentioned that girl on the crazy horse to her. I mean, why stir up trouble?

Fire in the Hole

Vercil he seemed a mite queer, nearing sixty in age, countrified in upbringing and appearance, not burdened by any discernable occupation. He might have escaped public notice had he not elected to become a gopher, felt the call, opted for rodenthood, told his wife, Purlie, he didn't give a damn what anybody thought, succumbed to subterranean flights of fancy.

Purlie, she wasn't no prize, neither. Feisty in a skinny and wrinkled way, smoked a corncob pipe, always giving Vercil hell about something. She'd light into him, stand square in front of him, take the pipe out of her mouth, start jabbing Vercil in the chest with the stem while she blasted him about whatever was on her mind at the time. Usually it had to do with turnips, purple-topped roots from the garden, a favored food of her husband, tangy and crisp but gas generating. She didn't like the smell of it, she didn't like the sound of it, she told him plain he was a disgrace to human society.

The morning Purlie came out of the house and saw the pile of dirt in the back yard she stood in wonder for a time, eyeballed that four-foot-high mound of fresh moist earth, noticed the sewer-cover-sized hole next to it, caught the pipe as it dropped from her gaping mouth. Next thing she noticed was an entire row of turnips missing, neat spherical cavities marching in precision, a major vacancy in the garden, conundrum added to conundrum.

She approached the yawning hole, bent low for a better look, cocked her head first one way and then the other, realized it was Vercil at work in his new personna. "Vercil, you no account varmint, are you down there?" She listened, she waited, she grew impatient.

Purlie straightened, her brow creased in thought, perplexed for a while, at last shrugging in acceptance of the hand fate had dealt her. She tamped tobacco in the pipe bowl, fished a kitchen match from her apron pocket, struck fire to the corncob. Still in a state of cognitive reflection, she tossed the flaming match into the hole, felt the rumble as methane ignited, the earth lifting and settling back in place. Said, "Well, I'll be damned," when Vercil was expelled from the bowels of the earth like a smoking mortar round engulfed by flame.

Vercil landed birth naked in the yard, face and knees against the ground, in the prayerful attitude of Islaam, of which neither he nor his wife had no knowledge, his singed body inert in death. Not a follicle sprouted on his once hirsute form, skin blackened in piebald blotches, a pale yellow flame issuing from his upraised posterior, glowing testimony to flatulence and human vacuity.

Purlie stood in awed admiration, the last dirt clods dropped from the sky, the five-inch flame diminished to pilot-light proportion, her heart fluttered with pride, the flame wavered and went out. "Lord be praised!" was her cry. To have been witness to such a singular event, to feel the glory of it, to be part of something not seen every day.

My Brother's Keeper

It's one of the eternal truths of the universe that no good deed goes unpunished. Do-gooders are vilified no matter how pure of heart. Take my brother, Varner. He's an attorney. Has a thriving law practice over in Hebron City. The last week of October Varner's wife, Sissy, left him and took their two kids with her. None of us in the family knew what the trouble was, and Varner wouldn't talk about it.

Sissy fit into our family from the very beginning like she'd always belonged. Mom and Dad loved her like one of their own, and if Varner hadn't caught her first I'd have married her in a New York minute. Their split-up hit us like a death in the family. An aching void remained, a key element missing.

The third week of November Dad phoned. "Son, are you going to be able to make it down for Thanksgiving this year?" They live in a Dallas suburb, about a five-hour drive from here. "Sissy and the kids'll be here for the weekend." The way he said it, I knew there was something more. After a pause he added, almost in afterthought, "Why don't you bring Varner? Maybe something good will come of it." Right. Varner is stiffnecked proud and not apt to be overjoyed with the rest of us tinkering in his personal affairs.

Good old Dad. Mr. Fixit. He offered no advice, none whatsoever, on how to go about enticing Varner to attend the festivities. After stewing overnight about the situation, stealth and cunning seemed the best approach.

Varner answered his phone in a surprisingly buoyant mood. "I bought the car I've always wanted, Bud." He always calls me Bud. "I had a nice personal-injury settlement the other day, and I found this completely restored MG roadster. It's a beaut."

"Well that's dandy, Varner. Since my truck has come up lame maybe you can run us down to the folks for Thanksgiving." I drive a fourteen-year-old pickup that has a grocery list of infirmities.

It was like I'd just announced his appointment to the Supreme Court. "Terrific, Bud. I've been wanting a chance to try her on the road. I'll pick you up about four Thursday morning. That'll give us plenty of time to get there by dinner." Sometimes you worry for nothing. Things couldn't have worked out slicker. There didn't seem to be any need to mention Sissy and the kids.

True to his word, Varner pulled into my driveway before the first rooster crowed. It was a cute little car, alright, with the big headlamps and a shiny square radiator. No telling what that automobile cost him, but Varner always had a talent for making money.

We merged from the off-ramp onto the interstate at a higher rate of speed than seemed prudent. "Aren't we headed the wrong direction, Varner?"

He grinned like a kid with a new wind-up toy. "I thought we'd take Route 7. You know, get off the interstate and enjoy the scenery, give this baby a workout." He could hardly be heard above the wind and road noise. Those cars sit close to the ground, and the rag top had a flutter to it.

After sixty miles of accelerating through turns and the growing likelihood of me losing breakfast, we came to the town of Dulcet. If Varner saw the 30-mile-zone sign he didn't let on. We passed the business district, a combination feed store/gas station/grocery, in a blur. Our headlights focused on a rapidly approaching yellow diamond-shaped sign with a crooked black arrow on it. "Watch this," Varner said and attacked the "S" curve with aggressive abandon.

Oyster-colored pre-dawn smudged the black eastern horizon, dividing it from the darkness overhead. An early-rising farmer, his house on one side of the highway and his cattle pastured on the opposite side, stopped his pickup truck on the narrow blacktop while he got out to open the pasture gate. The truck, piled with baled hay, a farm dog riding on top, loomed in our light beams when we squealed out of the turn.

The sequence of events following impact are not firmly fixed in mind, but a flying hay bale stripped the canvas top off the MG. A broken bale and the dog followed, filling the cockpit area with a tangle of stems, leaves and snapping teeth. The farmer ran up to my door, eyes wide with excitement. "Are ya hurt? Are ya hurt?" Come to find out he was talking to the dog.

We escaped serious injury except for Varner being dog-bit some. The car was a mess, for sure would never run in competition anyways soon. Varner stared at the cloud of steam rising from the crumpled front end and emitted a stream of colorful imagery that would put a heavy-equipment operator to shame. And him a deacon in the church.

It was nearly an hour before a state trooper got there and wrote up everything, another hour before the tow-truck arrived. We hitched a ride into town with the wrecker. Varner gave the driver $200 to borrow his personal car, an eight-year-old greasy Chevy Caprice that sagged on one broken spring.

Varner stopped at the first liquor store we saw and came out carrying a pint of something that had "Kentucky" on the label. "You drive, Bud." He slid into the passenger seat and didn't speak to me again the entire trip. He did carry on an unintelligible, running conversation with the bottle.

We arrived on our parents' doorstep mid-afternoon. In spite of my efforts to unobtrusively support Varner by one arm, he listed badly when we made our entrance. The family had finished dinner but remained seated around the dining table. The children reacted first. "Daddy, Daddy!" They ran with outstretched arms to greet their father who went to his knees, fell actually, and embraced them. I winced at the thought of those sweet babes encountering their daddy's breath.

Sissy wasn't far behind. She strode with purposeful steps toward the reunion. Her eyes said she'd accurately assessed her husband's condition, and she was showing fight. "Varner, how could you? How could you do this to your children?" Tears, either from joy or the fear of imminent domestic violence, coursed down Varner's cheeks. I stood back proudly, my mission successfully concluded.

Then Sissy turned on me. "How could you let him get in this condition? Your own brother. How could you?" With me to vent her anger on she apparently had a change of heart about her husband. She helped Varner to a more-or-less upright position, threw his arm around her shoulder and started down the hall with him toward the bedrooms.

Dad, voice filled with regret, said, "How could you let him do that, Son?" I looked to Mom for help and received only a disapproving frown. Varner's four-year-old boy, Buster, kicked me on the shinbone. Why is it in our society that people fall all over themselves with sympathy for a penitent drunk but attack innocent bystanders? I'd had enough.

"Dad, I'm going to fix myself a quick sandwich, then I'd appreciate it if you'd take me to the bus station."

That's how I came to be riding a Greyhound north on I-30 on Thanksgiving Day. My knees firmly clasped a bottle-shaped brown paper bag between them. I sat surrounded by what I guessed to be an extended family of eight or nine people, only one of whom spoke English. The ample, middle-aged lady in the aisle seat next to me repeated one comprehensible sentence. Every time I lifted the brown bag to my lips she threw a baleful glare my direction and said, "Shame on you, Senor."

Scars

Sitting here in the half-dark with Garth Brooks singing at me, it might be the haze of stale cigarette
smoke causing my eyes to water. It might be that,
but then again it might be something else. I'm wondering how I come to be at this table in a North Little Rock
bar. Me, Elzie Timmons, who don't hardly ever even go
into bars. Look at me, working on a bottle of beer, the
number of which I already lost count. Jukebox music's
pounding, but it's not near loud enough to drown out
the voice that keeps worrying at me. Why did I ever
bring her into this place? It might have been a accident,
but again, maybe it was meant to be... just maybe, it
was meant to be.

You see, it's all on account of a woman. I never met
anyone like her in my whole life, and now she's gone.
Walked right out that door over there and left me trying
to fix a broke heart by pouring Budweiser on it. You ever
try that? I'm here to tell you it don't work worth a darn.

This all started one morning awhile back when I
stopped off at the Waffle House for breakfast. I was going to work like I do every morning except on Sundays
when I'm off and I can sleep late. I been working as
a roofer for Buster Goins. Buster, he runs a three-man

crew and he has work for us most all of the time. He don't get any of them big, new subdivision jobs, but he works cheap and there's always somebody needing a new set of shingles on account of there's been a windstorm or maybe the roof is old and just starts in to leaking for reasons nobody knows about.

When I walked into the Waffle House that morning I saw right off they had a new waitress. The counter seats were filled up and I had to set at one of them little window tables that's not hardly as big as a spread-out newspaper. The napkin holder and the salt and pepper shakers and the cream and sugar packets and the Tobasco sauce bottle with the toothpicks takes up most of the room and it's all you can do to eat a meal on one. I was trying to decide between eggs and bacon or a ham omelet. This new waitress I mentioned brings me a cup of coffee and pulls her pad out to write my order on it like they always do.

She's a pretty little blonde girl, the fact of which didn't escape my notice the minute I walked in the door. What I didn't see when I walked in was two things... no, it was three things; one, her eyes were brown, about the shade of flue-cured tobacco and, two, she had her a build that would stop traffic on the I-40 off-ramp and, three, she walked with a limp on account of one of her legs being shorter than the other one. The name-tag on her blouse said Ruthie.

"Are you ready to order?" she asked me, her voice soft and kind of timid sounding like she was afraid she was going to be yelled at. There wasn't no smile on her face and she seemed nervous like waiting tables was a new and trying experience for her. I never thought much about it before but I couldn't see anything about

Loose Ends

waiting tables to make a person nervous. You just find out what it is people want and then you bring it to them. It's not exactly like nailing shakes seven inches to the weather on a hip roof.

"Yes, Ma'am," I said. I give her a smile and tried to look friendly which ain't always easy for me to do because I have a face that's been known to scare little children. I was in a car wreck nine years ago when I was fourteen, and my face went into the windshield sudden-like. It left me with this long purplish scar down one cheek that's mashed in some on account of broken bones that couldn't be straightened out all the way. That was before I learned to buckle-up when I got into a car, which I've made a habit of doing ever since.

"I believe I'll have the ham omlet," I said, giving her the benefit of my lop-sided grin. She wrote it on her pad and I could see her taking a couple of quick looks at my face, the bad side being turned toward her. She hurried off without saying anything else, and I felt a kind of ache for her when she hoppity-skipped back behind the counter.

You see, she had a lost and hunted way about her that made me want to hold her and comfort her. I didn't have no idea that she needed holding and comforting, but that was what was in my mind. When I was a boy a stray Beagle pup showed up in our yard. Hair full of burrs, ribs like a Jeep grill, it cringed on the ground whining at me. The tender feeling I had for that pup was what I felt about Ruthie. I've seen lots of pretty girls in cafes and places, the way you always do, but this was the first one to give me a case of the flutters, like I had then. It wasn't altogether that I felt sorry for her, which I did in a way, it was because her having a

Loose Ends   127

gimpy leg seemed to make the rest of her that much more beautiful. You know what I'm saying? It's like finding buttercups in the pasture growing in the middle of cow pies. Well, maybe not exactly like that, but you see what I mean.

I never had much to do with girls, and girls never had much to do with me on account of my face being the way it is. Even girls who seemed friendly were out of reach to my way of figuring. All I could think about when I was talking to them was that bodacious purple scar I knew they were looking at. But somehow my face didn't seem so important when this girl, Ruthie, was standing next to me.

It wasn't but three or four days before Ruthie begin to smile at me in the mornings. I'd say things to try to get a conversation started, like, "It looks like it's going to be a nice day," and she'd just smile and wouldn't say nothing except, "Are you ready to order?" But I had the feeling that she was glad to see me even if she was too bashful to let on.

Well, finally, I asked her for a date and she agreed. We took in a movie and neither one of us said much that first time. We looked at each other a lot but couldn't seem to get the conversation past "It sure was a good movie" and "Yes, it was." Then talking got to be easier for us the second time. We set over coffee after the show and it was like one of those frog-strangler summer rains the way she opened up. She told me how I was the first man she ever felt comfortable enough with to go on a date, how when she was in school kids would mimic her walk and how she'd been afraid all her life that people would laugh at her — — things like that. I almost cried listening to her because I knew plenty about those same kinds of feelings and about lonesome. Me and lonesome were well acquainted, I can tell you, and just being with Ruthie made that by-yourself feeling fade right out of my mind.

Ruthie and me became lovers before long. She said we couldn't never go to her house on account of her daddy and mama being there, so we always went to my place. It's a rent trailer I pay $275 a month for in Landers' Mobile Home Park. The trailer's old and just ten-wide by forty, but she didn't seem to mind any of that. She told me her heart was overflowing with joy; overflowing being the word she used, and I know my heart was, too. We never talked about our disabilities during our times together. You crawl into a bed with Ruthie and disabilities would be the last thing to cross your mind.

We went on like that for several weeks. I'd pick her up when I got off work, and maybe we'd go to a movie or maybe we'd just go straight to my place, depending on our state of mind at the time.

It was one of those times when we were at my place, just laying there relaxed and enjoying the quiet and the nearness of each other when she said, "Elzie, you've made me a different person." I turned on my side and looked at her, wondering what it was she meant. "Before you started talking to me at the Waffle House and asked me for a date, all I could think about was how ugly I was and how somebody might laugh at me. I never thought anybody could love me." She put her arm around me right then and pulled real close. "I used to cry at night thinking I'd never know what it was like to be with a man. You changed all that for me. Thank you, Elzie."

I tell you, it made me feel important somehow, even valuable, feelings the likes of which I'd never had before. That was one night I won't never forget.

Ruthie wasn't the same shy little mouse that she was when we first met. I could see by the way she smiled and talked to customers at the Waffle House that she had a higher opinion of herself than she did before. I'd changed some, myself, and I was giving some serious thought to marriage.

It's funny how we came to go dancing that night... I mean tonight. It just seems like it was a long time ago. We were in my truck at the time, just cruising around with the windows down, enjoying the night air, and she told me she'd never drank a beer in her whole life. I pulled in at The Lucky Spot on account of it being the first bar we came to and it having that big ace of spades up on the front in neon lights and all. We set in the truck a minute just listening to some old lonesome Merle Haggard song drifting through the windows from the jukebox inside. She said to me kind of wistful-like, "Something else I've never done is dance." I tell you, it almost broke my heart to hear her say that. I never thought about it before, but here was a girl twenty years old, feeling the music inside her all her life, wanting to dance but too shy and too scared to do it. I came near to crying.

It was crowded inside, crowded and noisy and kind of dark, and several couples were dancing in a space that wasn't hardly as big as the living room in my trailer. We found us a table and I went to the bar and got us a couple of Buds. Ruthie set there nursing her beer, kind of getting used to the taste of it and all. That fiddle and guitar music was playing and couples were whirling and stomping, having theirselves a good time. Ruthie was watching them, smiling, seeming to enjoy herself, and directly she said, "I want to try it, Elzie. Let's you and me dance." Well, that just shows you how much she'd come out of her shell. I guess I was more nervous about it than she was, seeing how I wasn't much of a hand at dancing, myself.

I took her by the hand and led her out among the other couples. I held her close to me with my arm around her, and at first we just stood there swaying to the music, letting the beat kind of grow on us. It was kind of awkward when we started moving, on account of her dipping down and then up every other step, but pretty soon we got the hang of it and we whirled around like the rest of the people were doing. Ruthie's eyes were lit up and her smile just about tore my heart right out of my chest.

It was right then I felt somebody tap me on the shoulder, and this cowboy fella wearing a black hat says, "Mind if I cut in, Podner?" Hell yes, I minded, but I didn't say nothing, just stood there and watched while Ruthie, still smiling, went into his arms without missing a beat. I felt like a cedar post standing out there in the middle of the room by myself, so I edged back off the dance floor.

That was when I noticed the cowboy had one leg shorter than the other. His was opposite of Ruthie's, and the two of them looked smooth as silk out there on account of both of them dipping at the same time. It was beautiful to see. I mean, I was feeling like the third pig at a two-pig trough, but them two danced like they was welded together. First thing you know other couples were standing back watching them. Ruthie was so beautiful and happy looking people couldn't take their eyes off her.

They just kept on dancing, one record right after another. Bad as I wanted to, it just wasn't in me to go out there and cut in on them. I could tell Ruthie was having the time of her life and I didn't want to spoil it for her. I got me another bottle at the bar and went back to our table where Ruthie's beer was getting flat.

After about forty minutes and one more beer, Ruthie and the cowboy stopped dancing and stood there on the floor with their heads together talking for a minute. Then she came by herself over to where I was setting. She stood there and looked at me with a kind of sad smile, and I got this sick feeling about what was coming. Finally she laid her fingers gentle-like on the bad side of my face and she said, "I'm sorry, Elzie," and she left. Just walked over and took that old boy's arm and they went hippity-hopping out the door, the two of 'em out of sync on account of both of their outside legs being short.

My hand went to my cheek where Ruthie'd touched it, and I set there all hollowed-out inside, trying to remember the touch and the sight of her. It come to me how a gambler must feel when his lucky streak runs out. He sees all his winnings being raked in by the player on the other side of the table, in this case a gimp-legged cowboy in a black hat, and he realizes that making the big kill was all a dream — — a dream he fooled himself into believing.

That was nearly three hours ago, and I'm still looking for salvation in a amber bottle. I keep thinking they might come back, and she'll set across the table from me and tell me it was all a mistake on her part and ask me to take her home. But there doesn't seem to be much reason to hang onto those thoughts now, the bartender telling me to drink up on account of he wants to close.

I believe I'm gonna give Shoney's a try for breakfast in the morning.

Call Me Jerry

I manage the Beefy Burgers drive-in here in Hargrave. It's the only place in town to eat except Polly's Southern Cooking down the street. You want to stay out of Polly's. It's a wonder the health department hasn't closed her down. They might do it, too, if her uncle wasn't the inspector.

Hargrave's not much of a town, just four blocks of businesses strung along one side of Route 27, the MoPac railroad being on the opposite side. The lunch crowd from the chicken-processing plant keeps me going. There's a couple of hundred people, mostly women, works there. On noon break they swarm this place like ants on a doughnut.

Tuesday my assistant cook, Vernon, quit. Took off with some old gal from the plant he was living with. Said she'd got plumb tired of eviscratin' chickens and the two of 'em was heading for Texarkana to look for work in the city. That's why I had the HELP WANTED sign in the window.

You know how hard it is to find decent help nowadays? It ain't easy. Kids show up here with their hats on backwards and rings in their noses, looking for a way to earn a few dollars for meth or grass. They all got attitude problems. None of 'em wants to work.

Maudine stops in yesterday and asks for a job. She's a farm girl, real polite. I tell her she can start this morning and I take the sign out of the window. She gets here a few minutes before nine, driving her daddy's truck. She parks on the far corner of the lot, gets out and slams the door hard enough to raise dust. There's enough mud dried on the wheels, bumper and hood to grow a garden.

"Morning, Maudine. Are you ready to go to work?"

She has kind of a bashful smile. "I'm ready whenever you are, Mr. Poulson."

"Call me Jerry, Maudine. Come on back, and I'll have Kyle get you started." Kyle, he's my cook. Big fella. Round red face hanging out of a white towel he wears around his neck. Kyle, he sweats a lot.

Maudine follows me into the kitchen. I introduce her and Kyle and tell him to get her an apron and show her the ropes while I unload the delivery truck.

About an hour later, after stocking hamburger patties, produce and such, I find Kyle taking a smoke-break out back. He's sitting on a garbage can, wearing a white cap and a stained apron over a stretched-thin white tee-shirt with body hairs sticking through. "What do you think, Kyle? Is she worth keeping?"

He blows two streams of smoke out his nose and grins at me. "She's a worker, I'll say that for her. Chops onions like a Chinaman." He wipes the end of the towel across his forehead and makes a face. "But man, she puts the U in ugly." Kyle, he's plain-spoken, but he has a point. Maudine's mousey-colored hair frames a too-slim hatchet face and lantern jaw. Her boney nose barely keeps her eyes apart, and her complexion needs work. "From the back she looks right interestin'," Kyle continues, "but when she turns around she makes time stand still." He grins before he finishes the ancient joke. "Her face'd stop an eight-day wind-up clock." He rambles on, using all his similes for homely. Mud fence. Hogan's goat. Bucket of pliers. Twenty miles of bad road.

I turn away, cutting off his colorful recitation. "I'm glad to hear you two are getting along, Kyle. Keep up the good work."

Lunch is the usual madhouse. "Two chili-dogs with extra onions, fries and a medium Pepsi." "One double Beefburger, onion rings, fried apple pie, large chocolate shake." I work the drive-through window and keep an eye on Maudine in the kitchen.

Most new help gets rattled when the noon crush hits. Not Maudine. She is calm as the Virgin Mary, grabbing orders off the wheel, ladling chili, bagging burgers and fries like she'd done it all her life. Working the grill, Kyle towels sweat off his face and glances at her with respect, maybe awe.

We clean up after the rush is over, sit at a window table eating our own lunch. I notice Maudine's truck setting in full sunlight on the far corner of the lot. A wisp of smoke rises from the bed. Halfway across the parking lot I can tell it's a cloud of flies and I can hear the buzzing. A rank smell greets me as I get closer. Piled hap-hazzard in the bed, one tossed over another, are four dead Holstein calves, tongues hanging out, green flies ringing their eyes, in their noses. It's a mess.

Maudine follows me across the lot. She leans her arms on the tailgate, studies the arrangement in the truck bed. "What are the calves for, Maudine?" I'm trying to be easy with her, not too judgmental.

"They're for Daddy." She braces her hands on the tailgate and hikes one foot up on the bumper, casual like. "He raises huntin' dogs and this cuts down on his feed bill some. I pick 'em up at Egstrom's dairy once a week."

"Well, Maudine, do you suppose you can do that after you get off work from now on? Our customers are common as dirt, but there's some things even they won't put up with."

She turns facing me, looking more puzzled than hurt. "Sure, I can do that, Mr. Poulson. I reckon some folks are skittish about the strangest things."

"Call me Jerry, Maudine." We start walking back across the lot. "And if you don't mind, Maudine, keep parking your truck in that same place."

Several days pass, and Maudine proves to be the best hand in the kitchen I've ever seen. She cleans while she works. Never leaves a mess behind. When the rush hour ends the only cleanup left to do is wiping down the work tables. Cheerful and industrious, she makes everyone's job easier. A nicer person you'd never want to meet.

Whenever I check in the kitchen, and that seems to happen more and more often, I find some reason to stand close to her, and she doesn't seem to mind. I realize right off there is more than an employer/employee relationship working here. She is still homely as a patchwork quilt, but I don't think about that much anymore.

Me and my wife split the blanket two years ago and I swore off women. But Maudine brings about a change in me. My mind isn't concerned with her looks when she stands close. I find myself thinking about the gentle way she speaks, how she cares for people's feelings, mine in particular, and how nice it would be to have someone share my empty apartment.

Still, when I began to consider asking her out, I can't help thinking about where we'd go, what we'd do. Do I really want to be seen with her at the movies or in a restaurant or shopping at Walmart? It takes some time for me to decide I can handle that, the benefits weighing greater than any possible embarrassment.

So I ask her. I walk out to her truck with her after work. "Maudine, how would you like to go over to Pottsville with me this evening and take in a movie?" I figure it'll be dark when we get there, and we won't be noticed much.

She gets in her truck and shuts the door. Without expression she looks at me through the open window. "I appreciate you askin' me, Mr. Poulson, but I'm afraid not." That's not what I'm expecting to hear. Not at all.

For a few seconds all I can do is stare at her close-set eyes, trying to figure where I went wrong. "Do you mind telling me why, Maudine?" I'm hoping there's some way I can change her mind.

She starts the truck and shifts into reverse. "This'll probably cost me my job, but to tell the truth I don't want my friends to see me with you."

Let me tell you, that hurt. "Why's that, Maudine?" My voice doesn't want to work right because of the pain I'm feeling.

She leans out the window and starts backing the truck real slow. "You're overweight and going bald. And besides that, you dress like a carnival barker. Goodnight, Mr. Poulson."

I watch her drive out of the lot, look down at my plaid pants then mutter to no one in particular, "Call me Jerry, Maudine."

The C-n-C's Woman

Jack Lynaugh's Shamrock Pub, John D. Lynaugh, proprietor, is a favored watering hole for newspaper and television people. Located at Fifth and Montgomery, it's where I eat most noontime meals, conduct a lot of my business. I'm a reporter for The Record, two blocks east of the pub on Montgomery Street. Lynaugh's is a place, no matter how many times you've been there, that invites your admiration as soon as you walk in the door. Ornately designed tessellated floor, square tables under red-checkered tablecloths and curved-back wooden chairs are right out of the 19th century. A thirty-foot mahogany bar, with carved paneled front, supports polished brass foot and top rails. No fancy upholstered stools, this is a bar where gentlemen stand, foot on rail, while partaking of their nectar of choice. Overhead brass light fixtures reflect in the center mirror behind the bar. Carved wooden cabinets and shelves line the back wall and contain the potions dispensed to Jack's clientele.

About nine-thirty Monday morning I walked in and paused for my usual appreciative survey. Jack, neat and trim in his white barman's jacket, stood behind the bar, drying a glass with a towel. It was too early for the drinking trade, but Jack was always good for a cup of coffee and a little baseball talk. "Top o' the mornin', Jack." It's not an original greeting, but I like to play at being Irish.

Jack smiled, set the glass on a shelf. "Sure and it's my favorite muckraker. How are things this morning, Quint?" That's me, Quinton Reginald Baker. I know, it's a helluva name, but I'm stuck with it.

"Couldn't be bet…" The phone on the end of the bar rang and Jack moved to answer it.

"Lynaugh's. He's right here—just a second." He handed me the phone with a wink. "Your boss."

An s.o.b.'s s.o.b, Thomas Jefferson Gilkey is the only black editor of a big city newspaper in this northeast section of the country. He came up the hard way, paid his dues and now runs The Record with an iron fist. "Quint, get your ass down here a.s.a.p. I'm looking at the clock right now, and if you're not standing in front of my desk in five minutes you'll be reporting for the Backwater Gazette." I stood there blinking while the dial tone cut off the witty response forming in my mind. This was typical TJ bombast, but I thought my interests might be best served if I honored his request.

TJ's desk accommodated a clutter of papers and folders which he manipulated with one hand while engaged in unilateral phone conversation. He slammed the receiver down, glanced at the clock and smiled. I hate it when he smiles because I know what follows is not always pleasant. He extracted an airline ticket from a folder and tossed it in my direction. "You've got a flight to Little Rock in three hours. Be on it. Better go home and pack a bag first, this may take a couple of days."

I picked up the ticket. "Are you going to tell me what this is about, TJ, or do I have to guess?"

He leaned back in his chair, hands clasped behind his head. No afro on this man. His tightly kinked hair was cut close and business-like. His size 18/36 shirt strained to encase a linebacker's torso and neck. The smile, a hint of amused sadism, was back on his round face. "We got a tip about another woman, a Marvella Tyson, who is ready to publicly accuse the President of an improper sexual relationship. She reportedly lives in a town called Pistol City. You fly to Little Rock, rent a car, locate this woman and get me an interview. Enjoy your trip."

"Pistol City? Pistol City? Tell me you're kidding, TJ." The phone rang and he waved me off like a bothersome gnat. I'd been dismissed.

I live alone in a two-story house my parents left me. The house, a relic of the late 1890's, is sandwiched tightly between two brick apartment buildings. Wood framed with wood siding and shutters, it's narrow, first-floor front porch is embellished with lacy, delicate wrought-iron work forged by a French artisan imported for that purpose. A matching wrought-iron fence encloses the postage stamp front yard, giving a look of elegance to a structure well past its prime. It also looks as out of place in its setting as a Little Sister of Charity in a topless club. I'm trying to sell it, but not many people are interested in a 100 year-old house on a forty front-foot lot that gets direct sunlight only during lunch hour.

I let myself in the front door, packed a bag, called for a cab and left a note for my cleaning lady.

My plane was routed through Atlanta. Changed planes and flew to Memphis. Changed again and flew to Little Rock in something that would have thrown a scare into Eddie Rickenbacker. The day was pretty far gone when I picked up my rental car, a very small Dodge sedan, and checked the map the girl at the <u>Frugal Rent-A-Car</u> desk had given me. After an eye-straining search I located my destination, a dot on the map identified in minuscule print. Maybe there'd be a motel in the vicinity.

Ninety minutes of driving in the dark on a two-lane state route flanked by pine forests brought me to the sawmill town of Pistol City, pop. 437. I wondered how it rated a dot on the map. The first business I came to was The _we_t Dreams Motel, a 1950's structure with peeling paint and a carport between each unit. On closer inspection, the flickering neon sign revealed the word "Sweet" in flaking white letters beneath the darkened tubing. I drove through town, nearly a quarter-mile in length, made a U-turn in front of a grocery/hardware store and returned to the motel, resigned to spending the night in a room I dared not think about.

The motel office, lighted by one bare, overhead bulb, contained a wooden desk and a chair occupied by a man so frightening in appearance I almost backed out the door. I couldn't tell how tall he was, but he must have weighed 250 pounds or more. He might have been 60 years old, bald bullet head, tanned with deep wrinkles, coarse, pock-marked nose — he could have been a central-casting executioner. He wore bib overalls over dingy underwear with white chest-hair curling from the vee-neck. The set mouth and hard gray eyes did not invite casual conversation.

"Somethin' I can do for you?" It sounded like a throat-clearing. His big meaty hands toyed with a ballpoint pen while he stared at my suit and tie with something akin to malice.

Loose Ends

"Uh, I need a room for the night." I was pretty sure I wouldn't stay here a second night even if it meant a ninty-minute commute.

"Sixteen dollars." He never changed expression, just slid a registration card toward my side of the desk.

I quickly filled in the essentials and pushed the card back toward him. I didn't see a credit card machine, so I tossed sixteen dollars on the desk. "I'm looking for a Marvella Tyson. Do you know where she lives?" This guy didn't look like the gabby type, but reporters have to ask questions.

He glared, flint-like, at me while I tried not to focus on the pot-holed terrain of his nose. After several seconds of tense silence he rasped, "End of the first street on your right." He jerked his thumb in what I hoped was the right direction.

"Thanks," I said lamely. I really didn't want to push him for any more information, so I asked, "Can I have my key?"

"Number four—it's not locked." He looked at me, deadpan, apparently in dismissal. I hurried out of the office without a key, hoping my room's screen door had a hook on it.

I was out of the room before seven the next morning after a groaning, tossing night on a mattress which induced no dreams, sweet or _we_t. I cruised slowly through town, hoping I had missed a café the night before. I hadn't. I bummed a free cup of coffee at the grocery/hardware store and bought a package of miniature doughnuts covered with powdered sugar. I asked the store proprietor about Mz. Tyson. He directed me back to the only street I'd passed, a rutted, hard-packed, dirt track leading from the highway between a Sinclair gas station and a Purina feed store.

About two hundred yards along the dusty street, while dodging softball-sized rocks and licking powdered sugar off my fingers, I came to a cluster of ramshackle buildings, one of which appeared to be a residence. The street ended at a pasture fence immediately beyond the buildings, so I reasoned this must be the lady's domicile. I parked in front of the sag-roofed house and approached the door. Before I could knock, two young men, each wearing a black Rambo tee-shirt, walked around the corner of the house, saw me standing at the door and immediately stopped.

"Hi," I said. They appeared to be in their late teens, both tanned and fit-looking. One of the boys grinned but neither spoke. "I'm looking for Marvella Tyson. Does she live here?"

The grinning one nodded his head yes. "She ain't here, though. Are you the law?"

"No, I'm not the law. I'm a newspaper reporter and I'd like to talk to her."

The other boy, the larger one, came alive and blurted, "This is about the President, ain't it? He was here. The President of the U-nited States was right here. You're goin' to write about it, ain't you? Me and Virgil can tell you plenty about him. He shaken hands with us." The kid was excited, like he'd just been named for a starring role opposite Madonna.

I looked at the first kid. "You said she's not here. Do you know when she'll be back?"

"She taken her a job in Hot Springs. Don't reckon she'll be back anyways soon." His eyes widened, his eager look matching his brother's. "Are you really going to write about her?"

"Yes, I'm going to write about her. Do you know where she is in Hot Springs?"

The bigger kid said, "Marvella, she's a dancer. Works at a nightclub—Pink Go-Go, or somethin' like that. She's our sister." Undisguised pride registered in his voice.

In this business, information is where you find it, and when a subject seems anxious to talk, a reporter should not pass up the opportunity to ask questions. "Tell me about when the President was here." I took a notebook out of my pocket and clicked my ballpoint in anticipation.

"He come here in '92, the summer before the election? Said he was on R&R." Both boys giggled before the bigger one continued in speech so rapid I had trouble getting the facts on paper. "I don't know how much rest he got, but he got plenty of recreation. You could hear them bedsprings all over the house." It went on like that for ten minutes. When one boy paused, the other took over, describing what apparently had been a holiday-atmosphere interlude for most of Pistol City's citizenry, not to mention the President of the U-nited States.

I decided I might as well meet the entire family while I was here, so I asked, "Are your parents at home? Could I talk to them for a few minutes?"

The youngest boy, Virgil, said, "We live with Grandpa and Grandma. They both here if you want to see them." He led the way into the house and indicated a doorway hung with a cotton, patterned drape. An old man sat on a cluttered brass bed, a five-string banjo across his lap, his left hand around a tabby cat. Balding and wearing spectacles, he had a full white beard reaching to mid-chest. A crumpled felt hat lay on the bed behind him. Above it, on the wall, hung a picture of a massive, dappled-gray Percheron stallion, posed as though in a show ring. Framed military service documents and a certificate of appreciation from the Moose Lodge clustered next to the horse picture.

The old man didn't rise, there was no chair in the room, so I stood in front of him and introduced myself. "My name is Quinton Baker. I'd like to talk to you about your granddaughter." I noticed his trouser cuffs were basted with yellow wool yarn.

"What say?" Geez.

I upped the decibels about 120 percent. "My name is Quinton Baker!!"

He cupped his left hand to his ear. "What say?!" Deaf as a rock.

I gave him a snappy two-fingered salute. "Nice to meet you, sir." The two boys watched through the flowered drapes and had to step back as I made my exit.

Virgil confided, "He don't hear too good."

"No kidding? How about your grandmother, is she around?"

I followed my two eager escorts out of the house and toward the adjacent buildings. An elderly woman, a large Bible in one hand, backed out the door of the first structure dragging a chrome-legged, red vinyl-covered kitchen chair onto the low plank step. She closed the door and sat in the chair, opened the Bible on her lap and gazed, as if in meditation, into the distance.

As we neared her, it became obvious the building served as a place of worship. A hand-lettered sign of about three-by-eight feet diminsion centered above the door. What appeared to be a scriptural verse, in uneven block letters, reminded me of the desk sign, PLAN

AHEAD. The verse was followed by what I assumed to be the name of the church, JESUS – IS – THE – NAME, followed by a painted cross.

The woman wore a plaid, open-necked, ankle-length, button-down-the-front dress with what appeared to be a man's white tee-shirt underneath. Her gray hair was drawn back in a bun, and serenity occupied the wrinkled face like a badge of merit.

I approached the step where she sat and cleared my throat so as not to startle her. She turned her head toward me with a brief smile. "Good morning, ma'am." She nodded in response. "I'm Quinton Baker. I've come to talk with your granddaughter, but since she isn't here, I thought maybe we could have a chat."

She lifted a cupped hand to her ear. Her raised voice thundered and echoed off the buildings. "What was it?!!!" The Lord is not always merciful.

I turned to the boys. "Let me guess — she don't hear too good, either." Two heads solemnly nodded as one. I beat a hasty retreat to the Dodge, unfolded the map as I drove, and had determined which way Hot Springs lay before I reached the highway.

A town in a setting of scenic hills and lakes, Hot Springs is a maze of crooked streets clogged with automobiles waiting for signal lights to change. The Thoroughbred racing season had ended, but tourist-crowded White Duck amphibious vehicles lumbered down city streets in an apparent search for water.

I found The Pink Go-Go south of the racetrack. The barn-like structure, with it's garish rooftop sign, sat well back from the highway amid two acres of blacktop paving. Two automobiles were parked at one end of the wooden structure. Inside, the manager, a jolly type wearing a well-filled blue jumpsuit, was not only willing to give me Marvella Tyson's address, he showed me a photograph of her. He seemed eager and determined to be included in whatever story I wrote. I assured him I'd do my best and made my escape after getting directions to her apartment.

My search took me to a seedy part of town—crumbling brick buildings, cracked concrete sidewalks. Her apartment was off a small court or cul-de-sac, the entry next to an iron fire-escape ladder descending from the third floor. I hadn't yet reached the door when it opened and the lady in question, burdened by more paraphernalia than I could immediately identify, exited with a small blonde girl in tow.

"Ms. Tyson?" I had stepped aside to allow her to pass. She gave me a furtive glance and continued walking. Not being put off easily, I kept pace with her and introduced myself as we walked.

She rounded the corner and stopped, unflinching blue eyes looking directly into mine. "You're a reporter?" I nodded and began taking inventory of what she carried. She wouldn't get a hernia from the weight of her clothing. Short shorts and a tight-fitting sleeveless top showed off a trim body and nice legs ending with bare feet in open sandals. A carryall bag looped over her left shoulder, the arm squeezing a 1:4 scale stuffed polar bear snug against her body. Another tote bag was clutched in the hand holding the bear.

"I understand you are about to make public charges against the President. Could we talk about that for a few minutes?" Shoulder-length blonde hair was pulled back from a face with prominent cheekbones and strong chin. She'd rate fairly high for looks among the lengthening list of the Chief Executive's accusers. I'd guess her to be in her thirties, although her life-style may have added a few years to her appearance.

"I was taking my daughter to the park. It's just a couple of blocks if you'd like to come along. We can talk on the way if you like." Her low-pitched voice had a pleasant, soft drawl that brought to mind magnolia blossoms.

I did some mental arithmetic and nodded toward the little girl. "Is she the President's daughter?" She looked to be about five years old, hair in need of combing, clutching a well-worn doll with one hand while hanging onto her mother's hand with the other. She didn't appear to be very happy.

The woman turned and began walking at the child's pace before she answered. "Yes. She's his daughter, and the DNA tests will prove it." This had turned into a thunderbolt kind of story and my adrenalin level was rising. I could already see my by-line on the scoop of the year. Well, maybe scoop of the month.

We reached the park, shaded grassy areas surrounding playground equipment, and sat on a spread blanket while the little girl repeatedly climbed a ladder and slid down the metal slide. Marvella, we were on a first name basis now, told me her life story and answered my questions with no hesitancy.

After twenty minutes I stood, anxious to get to a telephone and drop this bombshell on TJ. "So, at nine tomorrow morning your attorney will announce at a press conference that you are filing suit against Bill Clinton?"

She gave me a blank look, stared at me for a full ten seconds. "Who said anything about Bill Clinton?"

I know my face turned pale, I felt the capillaries squeezing dry, felt a tightness across my chest. "You don't mean...?"

The briefest of smiles registered on her lips, in her eyes. "That's right—the other one."

I walked in a daze toward my car, head down, trying to absorb what I'd just learned. It wasn't flattering. An experienced reporter spends twenty minutes interviewing a subject and they each are talking about a different person—unbelievable.

A teen-age kid in jeans and a cammy shirt brushed against me. "Hey!" he yelled. "Watch where you're going, jerk!" I turned in time to see his one-finger salute, his angry face and wondered half-aloud, "Why can't we have a kinder, gentler America?"

The Sunny Gardens Affair

Icould hear the telephone ring while I fumbled my key into my office door lock. Monday morning, eight o'clock, and I was looking forward to another eventless week as sheriff of Luthur County. I crossed to my desk, flopped down in my chair and rolled forward until I could reach the phone. "Sheriff's office," I answered without enthusiasm, figuring it was my wife, Ellen, with some tid-bit she'd forgotten to tell me at breakfast.

A woman's voice said, "Is that you, Carter?" Who else would it be in a one-man department? My name's Carter Haygood. I'm in my second term as chief and sole law enforcement officer of a township so far back in the country you just about run out of road before you get here.

I cupped my chin in my hand and said, "Yes, ma'am. Who am I talking to?"

"This is Marcella over at Sunny Gardens," Sunny Gardens being a nursing home out on the north side of town. Marcella Clark is the owner/operator of same.

"How you, Marcella?" I asked. "How's Perry feeling today?" Perry is Marcella's husband and the only decent mechanic within a half-day's drive. I'd taken my wife's Dodge to his shop for a new alternator Friday. Perry'd come down with the flu that very day and Ellen was after me about getting her car back. Women get nervous when they're afoot for very long.

"He's better this morning," Marcella said. "I told him to rest another day. He'll probably go back to work tomorrow." Damn. Ellen wasn't going to be happy with that news. "What I called about, Carter," Marcella continued, "was one of our patients claims she was raped last night."

I rocked back in my chair and blinked at the two-bulb overhead fluorescent light fixture, noticed an increase in the number of fly specks on the tubes and considered what I'd just heard. "Is this some kind of a joke, Marcella? Are you telling me one of them old ladies was raped?"

She sounded earnest. "It might not be a joke, Carter. Maybe you'd better get out here." There hadn't been a rape reported in the six years I'd been in office. Property theft, hunting out of season and sporadic mailbox bashing topped the list of major crimes in my jurisdiction. I headed out to the back lot to get my cruiser, that being a euphemism for a stock tan-colored GMC pickup truck the taxpayers furnish me. It's got a light-bar on the roof and LUTHUR CO. SHERIFF'S DEPT. stenciled in black paint on both doors.

Sunny Gardens sets on a acre patch of weeds with a graveled parking area in front. The one-story frame building with its row of high windows looks like a modern farrowing house but without the penetrating smell. I parked the cruiser up against the telephone pole that lays on the ground next to the building.

Marcella met me at the front door. She's heavy, Marcella is. She's put together in rolls — hips, stomach, bosom, jowls. Brings to mind one of those Mrs. Butterworth's plastic syrup bottles. Perry likes to say she's warm in the winter and shady in the summer.

She got right down to business. "Carter, Dovey Grisham claims somebody, in her words, took advantage of her last night—early this morning, most likely. This place is locked up tighter than Dick's hatband after nine o'clock, so it had to be one of the guests done it." We had stepped into her office which is right next to the front door. Marcella took a load off by hefting one hip onto the edge of her desk. "There's eleven women lives here and seven men," she went on. "I wouldn't have thought all of them old coots put together could muster the where-with-all for this kind of a crime. We might oughta notify Bob Ripley." Marcella has a humorous streak in her if you'll just watch for it.

"Maybe we better talk to Dovie first," I suggested. "She's not hurt, is she?" I had visions of somebody beating-up on the poor old lady. Dovie's feisty but she wouldn't hardly weigh ninty pounds.

Marcella shook her head, sending tremors through her rouged cheeks. "No, she seems to be alright; just a little dazed acting is all."

"Does she know who did it? Are there any men works here nights?"

She shook her head again. "The only man that works here is Jeeter Snopes. Jeeter does maintenance and cleans the floors, but he's out of here before dark every day." Marcella eased her bulk off the desk and crowded through the door past me. She started down the narrow hallway with me trailing along behind. "Dovie said she didn't know who it was," she said over her shoulder. "She has cataracts, you know. Her room is right down here—she can tell you herself." We passed a series of closed hollow-core doors with metal house numbers tacked on them until we got to 6.

Dovie is a spinster lady, never been married. She was in a half-sitting position in the cranked-up bed. She wore what looked to me like a crocheted bed-jacket and matching bonnet of maroon and gray stripes, about the color of the high school football team jerseys. I swear her cheeks were flushed rosier than a new bride's, and the sweetest smile was on her face. I started to tip my hat before I remembered I'd left it in the cruiser. "Good morning, Miss Dovie," I said, thinking this might be one of the best mornings in her memory from the looks of her.

"Is that you, Sheriff?" Her little bird-chirp voice seemed filled with gladness if I was any judge.

"That's right, Miss Dovie. You care to tell me what happened here last night?" I already felt like there wasn't any sheriffing to be done, but things being slow at the office I decided to let it play out.

She batted her eyelids; the coy look of a teenager on her first date. Her voice weakened in self-pity like she was describing arthritic pains. "He had his way with me, Sheriff. I was helpless to defend myself, and he..." She gestured with her hands to indicate her vulnerable state. "He just had his way with me." Poor old soul. I couldn't tell if the regret in her voice was for the act itself or because there might not be any more in the future.

"And you couldn't tell who it was?" I had a notebook and pen in my shirt pocket, but I didn't see any need for using them at this point in my interrogation.

"Well, I couldn't see him very good, of course, but I think I'd know him if he did it again." Her cheeks had colored more and the smile was back in place. What I took for eagerness crept into her voice. "Do you think you could have a line-up, Sheriff, the way they do on the TV?" Lord have mercy. Did she really think I would parade men through her room until she settled on one?

I reached over and patted her hand. "Now you know I can't do that, Miss Dovie. You just rest up now and I'll go talk to the other guests." I followed Marcella out into the hall and she closed the door.

"She seems to be taking it well, don't you think, Carter?" I'd never seen Marcella actually laugh, but I thought she might be close to it now.

"Yes, I'd say so, Marcella. Do you think we could get the rest of the guests together so I don't have to go through all this with each one of them? Maybe talk to the ladies first and the men after." I really didn't have much heart for this, but I figured it needed doing.

"Why don't you just go on down to the sun room at the end of the hall, Carter, and I'll get everybody rounded up." She turned and began opening doors while I headed down the hall, wishing to God I'd taken my boat out to the lake early this morning.

Ten ladies began to shuffle into the room in twos and threes. Some of them looked like they were up for the day while others had on chenille bathrobes and fuzzy slippers. There was a walker and a couple of canes among them, and the smell of lavender was prominent. Several greeted me by name, remembering the times I'd given a talk on crime prevention in Luthur County I expect. These folks at the home really could use more entertainment.

They all settled into chairs, clucking and quarreling like a flock of Buff Orphington hens sorting out their pecking order. I began in my best official voice. "Now ladies, I expect you all have heard what happened to Dovie Grisham last night." Heads dutifully nodded. "What I need is, if any of you heard or saw..." Lilly Bradford, Buck Bradford's widow, waved her hand in the air. Lilly is nearly senile and requires careful handling on occasion. "Yes, what is it, Miz Bradford?" I figured she needed to use the restroom facilities.

"He done it to me, too," she said. Lilly is a plain woman; straight white hair in a shingled cut, black horn-rimmed glasses, black sensible shoes, brown hose rolled down below her knees. She had a mustache that any fifteen-year-old boy would envy. Her arms were folded across her chest like she dared anyone to dispute her.

"Who done what to you, Miz Bradford?" I asked in as kindly a tone as I could. I hoped she didn't mean what I thought she meant.

"That same man forced hisself on me," she declared, her mouth set in a grim line.

"Last night, you mean?" I was dumbfounded, wondering what in the Sam Hill was going on in this place.

"No, not last night," she said, her voice peevish like I should have known better. "It was about two weeks ago, on Bingo night," she declared, like that would fix it firmly in my mind.

"How do you know it was the same man?" I asked.

"Well..." she ducked her head before she looked me in the eye again, "I'm just guessing he was the same one."

"Why didn't you report this before, Miz Bradford?" It was beginning to look like the matter might require a full-fledged investigation.

She glanced down and her face took on a shade of

pink I hadn't noticed before. "Well... it never hurt me none, and it seemed to do him a world of good." Some of the ladies tittered at this, a couple of flowered handkerchiefs fluttering up to cover their owners' mouths.

Well, I put the group through some intense questioning and it turns out there was a total of six women claimed they'd had the same experience. Not one of them could, or would, identify the perpetrator. I had my notebook out by this time, and near as I could tell there was an occurrence every two weeks, like clockwork, with no repeat performances and no complaints filed. I dismissed the ladies and told Marcella I was ready for the men-folks.

Danforth Billings was the first man into the room. Skinny and toothless with a hawk beak, he had bloody toilet tissue fragments stuck onto several shaving nicks. Eyes sparkling with mischief, he took a front row seat while the others drifted in behind him. Before I could begin Danforth says, "Did you find the weapon yet, Sheriff?" He reared back in his chair, mouth gaped open in a high-pitched cackle while he pounded his leg. The others joined him in the hilarity. I let them have their fun, whooping and hoo-rahing. Lord knows they had little enough of it—except maybe one of them.

"Now, Boys..." I began after they'd settled down some. "Boys, there's only one reason I'm out here today, and that's because one of you didn't say please." There was some elbow nudging and a few smirks. I eyed the bunch of them, one at a time, before I put the question to them. "I don't suppose the guilty party would be willing to own up to it?" I'm not sure what I expected, but it wasn't what happened next. Seven hands raised as one—seven gnarled, arthritic, liver-spotted, trembly hands. There wasn't a man in this room under seventy-five, several past eighty. I could see it wouldn't be easy breaking down this geriatric wall of solidarity.

I turned my back on them and paced a little circle, trying to think. "Now we all know," I resumed after facing them again, "that one of these ladies most likely would have mentioned the fact if there'd been seven men in her bed. Even Miz Bradford is not so far gone that she can't count past one. Unless we've got a twelve-week medley relay going here, somebody's not telling the truth." I was half exasperated with the entire lot of them.

Well, the upshot of it all was that nobody talked. They didn't try to lie about it, they just wouldn't say anything. I got to studying about the whole situation, and it come to me that these old people, even the ones not directly involved, had been blessed with a little excitement in their lives. Imagine living out your days cooped-up in a place like this, hearing the same stories day after day, seeing the same faces. Why, they'd just had a diversion dropped on them that would last for days—maybe months, depending on how long the perp could maintain the pace. God love 'em, why not? I headed for the front door.

Marcella hailed me as I passed her office. "Well, Carter, is the case closed?"

"The case is closed," I told her. "There's some things government shouldn't mess with, things better left to the private sector."

Marcella rocked in her complaining desk chair and grinned at me. "Well you know what they say, Carter. The older the fiddle, the sweeter the tune." She's something else, that Marcella is.

I reached to tip my hat, then remembered and dropped

my hand. I pushed the front door open and said, "Tell Perry I hope he get's to feeling better real soon."

The Favorite

Pa looked up from where he sat on the splintered wood steps. He spat a brown splatter of tobacco on the ground between his feet and muttered, kind of growly-like, "Here comes that son-of-a-bitch, Tyson." Mr. Tyson, he's the trailer park manager. He fusses at Pa about late rent, and Pa don't have much use for him. Another man walked beside Mr. Tyson. They kicked at grass clumps alongside the street like they'd lost something.

We were sitting outside that evening in the shade of the trailer. Inside was like an oven, air too thick and heavy to breathe. Humidity almost as high as the temperature, the way it gets here sometimes. I was perched on an empty ice chest, Digger at my feet. Digger's tongue lolled out, wet and pink and panting.

We live in a two-bedroom unit in Pine Forest Mobile Home Park. It's kind of a fancy name for a trailer park with a thin row of dusty pines down one side. Nearly two hundred trailers, most of 'em old and run-down, line the streets. Junk cars parked here and there, some in running condition, some with flats, a few blocked-up with honeysuckle growing underneath and crawling over the hood.

We moved in here after Ma left us. She took up with

some slick-talking salesman, Pa called him, and the girls went with her. Rosie's eight, and Bonnie's just six. I decided to live with Pa. I always was a favorite of his, and he needs somebody around to look after him sometimes.

This twelve-by-fifty is all the room me and Pa and Digger need. Digger's a fox terrier—smooth hair, tan and white spotted, no bigger than a minute. Smartest dog ever lived, I guess. I can yell, "Here, Digger," and slap my hands on my chest? Old Digger'll jump right up in my arms.

I can bend over and yell, "Up, Digger," and he'll jump up on my back slick as can be. He'll fetch a stick or a ball quick as you can blink.

Pa, he never much liked Digger. He just tolerates him on my account. When Pa gets drunk, and that's been pretty often since Ma left, I keep Digger away from him. One time Pa threw him right through the screen door. I didn't want that to happen again.

Pa always was a drinker. He lost so many jobs because of it that we've always been poor. Ma worked some as a motel housekeeper. That's where she met the salesman. Since she left, Pa only works a day or two a week. Some weeks he doesn't work at all.

Well, Pa kept eyeballing Mr. Tyson and the other man. They worked their way kind of slow along the edge of the street until they got even with us.

"What are you huntin' for?" Pa hollered. I don't think he cared much, but Pa always was curious about other people's business.

Mr. Tyson stopped and faced us. "Mr. James, here, lost his billfold this morning. He thinks it was along this street someplace."

I got to my feet and trotted toward them. Digger jumped up, ears all perked, and followed me. "Do you have a handkerchief or something that has your smell on it?" I asked Mr. James.

He looked at me a little bit, like he thought maybe I was nuts. Then he pulled a handkerchief out of his pocket.

"Let Digger smell it," I told him.

He squatted and held his hand out. Old Digger came over and sniffed the handkerchief, excited and all. I knew he was ready for another game. I pointed down the street and yelled, "Fetch," and away he went.

The grass along the street hadn't been mowed lately, tall enough to hide beer cans and plastic hamburger boxes. Digger stopped after a bit and looked back at me. I waved him on, and he kept running back and forth through the grass like he was hunting mice.

Then he barked once and looked at me. I yelled, "Yes." He picked up something and came tearing back to me. It was the wallet. He dropped it at my feet and began dancing around on his hind legs like he wanted to do it again.

I handed the wallet to Mr. James, feeling kind of proud. He opened it up quick and counted the money. A big smile came over his face. "By golly, it's all here."

I was feeling really proud then, until Mr. James opened his mouth again. "How much do you want for that dog?"

My jaw dropped down, and it took a few seconds before I could tell him, "Digger's not for sale."

"I'll give you a hundred dollars for him." He'd pulled a bill from the wallet and he held it toward me.

I guess I've never so much as touched a hundred

dollar bill before, but I shook my head. "He's not for sale," I repeated.

"Is that your best offer?" It was Pa's voice, coming from behind me. He'd probably started walking our way as soon as he heard money mentioned.

"No, Pa," I said, more pleading than anything else.

He didn't pay any attention to me, just spat and wiped his mouth with the back of his hand. "Is that your top dollar?" he asked Mr. James.

"Well, I was going to give the boy a reward… how about a hundred for the boy and one for the dog?"

"Please, Pa. Don't do it." I'm eleven. I quit crying several years ago, but I could feel tears puddling. I know how Pa is when it comes to money. "Don't do it, Pa. Please!"

Mr. James held out two bills, and Pa grabbed them so quick his hand was a blur.

I yelled, "Here Digger," and slapped my hands on my chest. I caught him on the run, and I headed past our trailer fast as I could leg it.

"You come back here, boy! Goddammit, you come back here!" He was pounding along, close behind me. I knew he wouldn't last. Sure enough, before I got to the next street back of our trailer, he'd pulled up, winded and mad as hell. When I was sure Pa had started back, I circled around and sneaked up behind our trailer where I could watch.

Pa came dragging into the yard, red-faced and blowing hard. Mr. James met him with his hand stuck out. "I want my money back. Right now."

Pa always was one for taking the moral high ground. He said, "No, sir. We had us a agreement. A deal's a deal."

"You didn't deliver the goods!" Mr. James yelled in Pa's face. "No dog, no money, and that's final!"

"That sounds fair to me," Mr. Tyson chimed in. "No dog, no money."

"Who invited you on this turkey shoot?" Pa yelled at Mr. Tyson. "This is between me and James."

"Well, I'm siding with Mr. James on this. Unless you want us to hold you down and take it from you, you'd better hand over the money."

Pa never was much for violence, unless he had a clear advantage. But he didn't give in easy. "What about that reward you were talking about? You trying to back out on that?" He still could win the last trick.

"Okay," Mr. James agreed, "but you damn sure had better give that to the boy."

Pa didn't answer. He just fished one of those bills out of his pocket, handed it to James and stomped off to the trailer.

Digger and me didn't go home until late. We walked around the perimeter of the park, watching the night settle on us. Digger chased a few fireflies. It was nice out that time of day, the night air cool enough to feel good on my face.

When we got back to the trailer, there was no sound and no light. Inside, I could hear Pa snoring. When I turned the light on over the stove I saw a brown paper bag on the kitchen table beside a half-empty quart whiskey bottle. Next to the bottle was a shoebox-size 12-pack carton of J. B. Scott's tobacco. Pa must have talked somebody into taking him to town.

One thing I noticed about that whiskey bottle, it wasn't the rotgut brand he usually bought by the pint. This was aged in the wood bourbon. And he never bought more than a single pouch of chewing tobacco at a time. I moved the paper sack, felt something in it. Inside was a handful of bubble-gum in twisted wrappers.

Pa hadn't forgot me. I always was a favorite of his.

Winter Weary

Twisted branches grope in vain appeal
to sullen flinty skies,
autumn warmth beyond their reach, a memory.

Immigrant arctic winds skitter parchment leaves
in fitful aimless paths
that meander to nowhere and beyond.

April's golden blooms, hope now dormant,
lie in earth's cold bosom,
a promise to be kept.

Let it Be, Let it Be

On the heels of snow and ice, spring's green fingers break
through, and I ask where you been so long?

A single daffodil bud triggers multi-hued visions still un-
seen but not so far away.

Ancient bones rejoice for one more vernal pageant and I
can almost believe in eternity.

Spring has sprang, there ain't no doubt.
Winter has left from here about.

Flowers bloomin' in their beds.
Yellows, purples, blues and reds.

Robins chirpin' in the grass.
A purty sight, you bet your shirt.

Groceries

Emmitt pushed the dark-stained swinging door open and eased inside the saloon. Three sixty-watt, fly-specked bulbs cast alternate pools of murky light in the shadowed interior. Unsure and hesitant, he remained by the entrance. Yeasty stale beer smells and the activities of idleness renewed long-forgotten memories.

He'd been known as a rounder in his youth, no stranger to taverns. When he returned from the Great War and married he'd gradually put all that foolishness behind him. It had been a long dry spell.

What in tarnation am I doin' in this place? He and his family had just this afternoon come into Lamont after six days on the road. They'd made camp under a cottonwood tree on a ditch-bank across the railroad tracks from the small settlement. Dessie asked him to walk into town and get a few things. "Why don't you go and see if you can find a groc'ry store? We ain't had fresh milk since we left home, and some taters'd be nice... and maybe some canned peaches. We could use a little salt, too." He'd heard guitar sounds when he returned past the beer joint and couldn't resist entering.

Down to little more'n pocket change, no job, don't know nobody here. In a week's time we could all be starvin'. Just thinkin' about it gives me the trembles. Back-to-back years of failed crops had driven them and hundreds like them from their sharecropper farms. He and Dessie and their four children traveled in a worn-out Hupmobile halfway across the country from Oklahoma to the San Joaquin Valley. Flat tires, chewed-up wheel-bearings, boiling radiator, sleeping beside the road, fixing meals over smoky fires — they'd endured it all. *By God, it was almost more'n a man could handle. Maybe a beer'd do me good.*

A bulging brown paper bag clutched in one arm, he shifted his gaze around the hazy interior. The music came from his left where a skinny, sallow-cheeked young man under a black cowboy hat picked at the strings of a much-traveled guitar. Two men in faded overalls, one wearing a tattered brown suit coat, sat on chairs in front of the musician. Elbows on knees, both idly smoked. Each sipped now and then from amber, long-necked bottles.

Blue smoke hung in stale air over three men perched in a row at a soiled, cigarette-burned bar. Emmitt ambled over to where they sat on backless stools, lifted the bag of groceries to the bar but remained standing. The fat bartender, clad in khaki work clothes and no apron, stepped a few paces to face him. A road map of red and purple veins spread from his plum-colored nose across the hills and valleys of doughy cheeks. "Howdy, neighbor. What'll it be?" A kitchen match rotated from one side of his slack mouth to the other.

A sign posted on the wall behind the bartender read: Western Beer 10¢, Eastern Beer 15¢. "Reckon I'll have one of them Western Beers." He slid two buffalo nickels onto the scarred wooden surface.

The bartender grinned. "They's more'n one kind of

Western, neighbor. You want a Lucky?" Emmitt nodded.

The man seated on the first stool peered at him through black-rimmed spectacles. His dark hair receded beyond a hand-sized patch of freckled scalp. Yellow strings attached to the round tag of a Bull Durham sack hung from a chambray shirt pocket. A short stub of roll-your-own dangled carelessly from one corner of his mouth, blue smoke curling under his glasses, giving him a one-eyed squint. "Pull up a chair." He grinned a yellow, toothy grin and indicated the stool next to him. "You must be new in these parts."

Emmitt threw one leg over the frayed cushion and sat. His hand reached out and grasped the icy bottle the bartender slid in front of him. "Just got in today." He took a long pull at the refreshing brew. *Godamighty. How long has it been since I had me a cold beer? Two years? More? This was 1937 — the last one must of been in '34 or '35.*

"Where do you hail from?" The bespectacled man rotated on the stool to face him. He didn't talk like folks Emmitt knew, but he seemed friendly enough.

"Out of Checotah, Oklahoma." He took another pull at the bottle, savored the taste of it then looked at his companion. "You been around this country long?"

"Going on twenty years, but I was born in northeast Oklahoma about a hundred miles from Checotah."

Emmitt's gnarled fingers dug papers and a Prince Albert can from his overalls pocket. He furrowed a paper between two fingers, tapped tobacco into it and rolled a smoke. He eyed his neighbor with renewed interest. "What kind of work ya doin'?" The match flared bright, fire eating into twisted brown paper.

The man turned on his stool to retrieve his own bottle. "Most of the time I make shipping boxes for the packing sheds. For grapes mostly, but that doesn't start until summer. Plums will start up in a few weeks, but they don't last long." He drank from his bottle of Lucky Lager before asking, "Do you have a job?"

Emmitt shrugged. "Ain't had time to look yet. A fillin' station man said D'Georgo might have somethin'."

"Well, good luck to you." He didn't sound real hopeful.

"Ain't there much work around here? You got a job, ain'tcha?"

"Yeah, but things are slow this time of year. It'll be picking-up in a month or so, but you might get lucky before then."

"Lord, I hope so." *Nothin' the fella'd said sounded encouragin'. Shouldn't have come into this place. Might need ever' thin dime I still got. But a man needed somethin' once in awhile to make him feel like a man.*

They finished their beers in agreeable silence, looked at each other with grins and ordered two more.

The guitar player finished the tune he'd been working on. He addressed the audience of two seated in front of him. "This here's a song of my own composition. 'Cotton Patch Heaven,' it's called."

Bony fingers began to strum and he sang along in a nasal tenor voice. Heart-rending, mournful words brought to mind the old trail song, "When The Work's All Done This Fall," about a poor dying cowboy, a long way from home, who was heartbroken he wouldn't see his mother before he cashed in. Come to think of it, the tune sounded a lot like "When The Work's All Done This Fall."

Guitar chords and exchanged bits of conversation whittled away the time and three hours slipped by. Emmitt had no idea how many beers he'd swallowed. He was drunk enough for his head to be unsteady and sober enough to know there wasn't much change left in his pocket. *Damned fool thing to do, drinkin' all them beers.*

He turned to bid farewell to his new friend and saw the stool was empty. *Prob'ly went outside to piss agin the back wall.* He eased off his perch and lurched toward the door, finding that it conveniently swung both out and in.

The night's cool darkness comforted him for a minute while he got his bearings. *Godamighty – the groceries.* He went back through the swinging door and returned toting the bag.

Head and legs wobbly, he began the journey back to camp, hardly a quarter-mile away. It reminded him of walking the ship's deck when his outfit was sent to France in '17. *It was good bein' young then – no hungry mouths to feed, nobody to give a damn if you got drunk.* He stumbled crossing the tracks, recovered his balance and continued his erratic trek.

Their campfire glowed twenty, maybe thirty yards distant when the sickness hit him. He sank to his knees, nausea sapping his strength. The brown bag fell from his arms and he sprawled forward to lay with his face against the cool roadside dirt. He raised his head and heaved. Uhh-h-h-h-uh. Cold sweat beaded his brow, his mouth tasted sour and the turmoil in his stomach wouldn't let up. Uh-h-h-h, again.

He rolled onto his back, breath coming hard. Slime clung to his mouth and chin, but his arms felt too weak to bother about wiping them. The stench of vomit filled his nostrils. When his eyes opened, two blurry figures stood silhouetted above him. They turned out to be his wife and his oldest boy.

Godamighty damn! Dessie and the boy hadn't neither one seen me like this before. His mind turned dark with anger born of guilt. *What the hell are you starin' at? Ain't you never seen nobody fallin' down drunk before? Oh, God! What are you doin' mad at them? It's you done them wrong. I'm so sorry, Dessie. So sorry. I wanted to be a good husband and provider and I failed you — the boy, too. Godamighty, I'm cryin'. I got to get ahold of myself.*

He lifted his head, wiped at his eyes and, for the first time, spoke aloud. "I was feelin' a mite poorly for a time, but I believe I'm some better now." The shame of it stung him. *I lost their respect. They seen me in my weakness, rollin' in the dirt and filth like a damned hog. How can I ever be a husband and father again?*

He rose shakily to his feet, Dessie holding one arm, the boy holding the other, and started toward camp. A recollection of mission made him resist the pull on his arms. He stopped, turned to his wife. "Dessie, I b'lieve I dropped them groc'ries."

The Center

The Albert Dodson Senior Citizens Center, named for a former congressman and constructed with federal funds, sprawled on a treeless lot on Beecham Avenue. A flat roof covered a recreation room, dining area, a kitchen and two handicapped-friendly restrooms one labeled LADIES, the other GENTLEMEN.

Farris Briscoe sat at a round table in the rec room. Across from him Darnell Tubbs shuffled a deck of cards with palsied hands. The shuffle misfired and blue-backed Bicycles skittered across the surface. "Great day in the mornin', Darnell. We'll be here 'til sundown before we get this game played." Farris was on a tear, up 20 points in the Casino game. At two cents a point, he could almost taste the cold Dr. Pepper he'd buy with his winnings.

"Don't get your bells in an uproar," Darnell retorted. "I'm doing the best I can." His liver-spotted hands dealt the cards, four down to Farris, four in the middle face up and four down to himself.

"Are you coming to the dance tonight?" Farris peeked at his cards and grinned. "That new activities coordinator will likely be here. She's a real eye-full."

Darnell snorted. "All the good it'll do you. I doubt she coordinates the kind of activity you're thinking about."

"I play first this time." Farris showed the ten of diamonds and gathered the ten of hearts, the deuce of spades and the eight of spades from the upturned cards in the middle. "Look at that. Read 'em and weep, Darnell, Big Casino and Little Casino both on the first trick."

They finished the game amid good-natured quarreling. Farris caught an ace and won the point for most cards, giving him enough winnings for his Dr. Pepper. He bought one for Darnell, too, just to ease the pain of his friend's bad luck.

"You better come to the dance tonight, Darnell." Farris held the red can to his cheek a moment, enjoying the coolness. "That little gal might put a smile on your face, get your blood stirring."

"My blood doesn't stir much anymore." Darnell sipped his drink. "I doubt if yours does enough to interest her. I know kids are cute at that age, Farris, but good lord she's barely out of college."

"Tell you what, Darnell. I'll bet a dollar I get a date with her."

"By gum, you're on." Darnell slapped his knee and chuckled. "Easiest dollar I'll ever make."

❄ ❄ ❄

Her name was Tiffany, Tiffany Scroggins. Dark hair tumbled to her almost bare shoulders. A clingy yellow dress gripped curves like a new set of Uniroyals. Right hand low on her supple back, Farris guided her through the steps of a dreamy Artie Shaw number. "You like this music, don't you Mr. Briscoe?"

"Call me Farris, Tiffany." He pulled her a tad closer.

"Big Band music has a sweet sound, and Artie Shaw's Stardust is one of the sweetest." He allowed his hand to slide down a half-inch. "You're a wonderful dancer, Tiffany. Brings back some great memories."

The music ended. She pulled back but held onto his hand. "What do you do for excitement, Mr. ...I mean Farris. Do you ever go horseback riding?"

"Not for a long time, but I grew up riding horses. Do you ride?" He believed he could peer into the depths of those dark eyes forever.

"I have two saddle horses. Would you like to ride sometime?"

His heart pulsed to a Latin beat, a Samba maybe. "I'm available anytime, Tiffany. Just name it."

"Make it Saturday morning then." She gave him directions to her place and a warm smile.

❄ ❄ ❄

Darnell pulled the heavy door open and stepped into Room 331 at All Saints Hospital. Farris lay elevated in the bed, right shoulder and arm encased in a cast, a bandage across his forehead. "Lord love a little duck, Farris, what happened?"

"I fell off, Darnell, I fell off."

"You mean the horse?"

Farris rolled his eyes. "Of course the horse. Jumped right out from under me."

Darnell pulled a chair to the side of the bed and sat. "Well tell me about your date. How was it, if I'm not getting too personal." He reached into his pocket. "By the way, here's the dollar I owe you. Never thought you could do it, to tell the truth."

Farris took the bill. "Darnell, when was the last time you had a roll in the hay? I mean an honest-to-goodness old-fashioned roll in the hay?"

"You don't mean…?" Darnell's jaw dropped, and he leaned forward, awe-struck.

"I do mean, Darnell, I do mean." Farris leaned on his left elbow and looked down at his friend, smiled at him. "It was beautiful, a religious experience."

"You mean like raising the dead?"

Farris' smile broadened. "Yeah, something like that. I'm a completely different man than you saw yesterday, Darnell, completely different.

Darnell eyed the cast, the bed, the bandage. "I can see that, Farris. I can see that."

Old Friends and Acquaintances

"Sh"he's just an acquaintance, Twila, that's all." Twila had me backed into a narrow space between the refrigerator and dinette table.

"Acquaintance my foot," she yelled, shaking a spatula in my face. "Acquaintances don't throw their arms around you and kiss you on the cheek."

I'd had the misfortune of bumping into Emma June Fredricks when me and Twila was at the mall, and Twila was showing fight. She gets all worked up about the least little thing. "Honey, you know I'd never sneak around on you. She's just a woman who needed help, and I happened to be in a position to lend a hand."

That just seemed to set her off. "I'll just bet you were in position, and we both know what that was, don't we?" She stepped back and seemed to catch her breath. "Harley," she said, "Harley, I ain't going to put up with this no longer. One of us is going to have to leave."

I was stunned. Shocked and stunned, I tell you. "Twila, honey. Let's don't be too hasty about doing something we'll both live to regret." It shames me to beg, but what else was there for me to do?

"Oh, don't worry about that, Harley, there may be just one of us left alive to regret it." She waved the spatula in front of me in a threatening manner. Twila could be so cruel at times.

Well, I had my work cut out for me. I began a week long sweet-talk campaign. Even brought her a bouquet of mums and snapdragons and the like. By Saturday night I was back in her bed even if she did limit me to the far half of the mattress.

By the end of the following week things seemed to be smoothing out some. I mean I wasn't walking on eggs, afraid I'd say the wrong thing every time I opened my mouth.

Friday night after work I suggested we go out for dinner, maybe drinks first and a dance afterward. She actually smiled. It was the first time in two weeks she'd looked at me without a murderous glint in her eye.

Buford's Bar & Restaurant was lit up and lively looking. Lot's of people out for a good time this night. We found a table for two in the bar, ordered and sipped sour mash while we enjoyed the jukebox music. Bob Wills' Take Me Back To Tulsa, I believe it was.

"Are you ready for another?" I asked. Twila smiled and nodded, so I stood and stepped over to the bar.

Before I could get the barman's attention I heard a braying female voice bellow, "Harley, you old sweet son-of-a-bitch. Where you been keeping yourself?" A pair of wet lips met mine when I turned around. A stout pair of arms squeezed me against the fullest bosom I've run across in a while. "Don't you remember me, Harley? Marvalene Huxley? Good Friday? Dirty Harry's in Fort Smith?"

I swear I had absolutely no memory of Marvalene or Dirty Harry. I turned to explain all that to Twila, but she was gone. The empty table and two empty glasses were there, but Twila had evaporated like high-octane gas.

I found her at home. She was in our bedroom throwing clothes into an open suitcase. "Twila, honey. Please, please, please, Twila, listen to me." Lord I hate it when I get all whiney and pleading. It's not manly, but I just can't help myself. "Twila, honey, you've got to believe me. I never seen that woman before in my whole entire life. Honest, Twila, I'm telling you the plain truth."

She turned to me and spoke in a very civil manner. "Harley, would you please carry my bag down and place it in the car trunk?"

I stood in the driveway and watched until her taillights turned the corner. I figured she'd go to her mama's for a few nights and then phone to talk things over. Sounded like a plan. Meanwhile why waste the evening? I headed on back to Buford's Bar to see if Marvalene could jog my memory about where we'd met.

Twenty-five Cent Peaches

L uthur's stomach rumbled. Trudging along the dirt field-road, bare feet kicking up puffs of dust, the imagined sight and smell of fried chicken made his mouth water. He couldn't remember not being hungry. There wasn't enough to eat when they'd lived on a rented farm in Oklahoma. There wasn't enough to eat on the long weary drive across half the country, and it wasn't much better here on this California farm where his father had found work.

Grownups talked about the Great Depression, how times were hard. Times had always been hard for Luthur. Small for his age, he'd been born with a harelip. The first day at his new school the teacher asked his name. He answered in a near whisper, "Nuthur Narver," and sank lower in the wooden seat of his desk. Perceptive and sympathetic, she asked him to print his name on a paper. Luthur Garver, it turned out to be.

At recess that first day Luthur moped in solitude under the shade of a chinaberry tree. Floyd, an older aggressive boy with a mean streak, approached him, a gaggle of friends trailing behind. Floyd taunted, "Nuther Narver, Nuther Narver." The other boys joined the chorus, "Nuther Narver, Nuther Narver." Luthur shrunk into himself, chin on his chest. The boys gathered the tough-skinned berries from under the tree and pelted him. Luthur ran for the safety of the classroom.

It had always been like that, Luthur thought as he walked the dusty road under a hot sun. Ragged overalls hung from skinny sun-tanned shoulders, and beads of sweat trickled from his uncombed mop of brown hair. Ahead of him a stout team of mares, haunches straining, pulled a wagon load of hay out of a stubbled alfalfa field onto the dirt road. Luthur trotted to catch up and hitch a ride on the sweet smelling hay. He clambered over the neatly stacked bales of alfalfa and pulled himself on top.

At the front of the load, looking down on the mares' broad backs, sat Lonnie Phelps holding the leather lines in his hands. Beside him, smoking a roll-your-own, lazed Farris Grimes, his helper. Both men lived in the farm's labor camp, four small shacks including the one housing Luthur's family. Lonnie glanced over his shoulder at Luthur standing behind him. He nudged Farris and winked. "Luthur, do you know the difference between a mule and a pillow?" Luthur shook his head no, a shy grin on his smudged face. Both men laughed. Luthur knew he was being teased somehow. He waited, his face blank. "I reckon you ain't old enough to know about that yet," Lonnie surmised. He nudged Farris again. "Tell you what, Luthur, I'll give you a quarter if you'll jump off into that water." Irrigation tail-water stood a foot deep against the road on the wagon's off side.

Luthur stepped to the edge of the load and peered at the brown water ten feet below. "Honest? Nou'll nive me a nwarter?" It was a frightening drop, but a quarter... A quarter would buy an RC every day for five days. Five Milky Ways. He'd never in his young life possessed a quarter all his own.

"Well, I reckon you're too scared to do it, but if you was to jump off in that water it'd be worth two-bits to me."

Luthur stared again at the water passing slowly alongside the moving wagon. His heart raced. A quarter. He had to jump. Arms flapping, he leaped from the hay bales and landed with a drenching splash. I did it, I did it, he thought, gathering his feet under him and spitting a mouthful of dirty water.

He slogged back to the road and ran to catch the wagon again. Hair plastered to his head like a drowned-out gopher, water dripping from soaked overalls, he climbed back onto the load. Luthur held his hand out, triumphant. Lonnie ignored him. Impatient, Luthur shifted from one foot to the other. "I numped. Nive me my nwarter," he begged.

Still not looking at him, Lonnie said, "You didn't jump right."

Righteous anger gave him courage. "Nod-nammit, nou promised. I want my nwarter."

"You never jumped right, boy, now get outta here."

Lower lip quivering, tears forming, Luthur climbed down from the wagon. Dark thoughts accompanied his disconsolate shuffle on the walk home. Oh, that Lonnie Phelps. Liar. Cheat. He'd promised a quarter, and Luthur swore to himself he'd get even... somehow.

His mother's kitchen offered nothing in the way of snacks except for a pan of three biscuits left over from breakfast. Luthur took one, bit into it and chewed as he made his way to his place of refuge.

A cotton field bordered the camp on two sides. Luthur slipped into the second row of lush foliage. Taller than he was, the plants shaded the furrows between the rows, providing cool shelter from an unfriendly world. He sank to the moist earth and watched honeybees work the pale pink and yellow blossoms among the dark green leaves.

The faraway sound of a John Deere tractor filtered to him above the bees' drone. Then he heard another sound, Lonnie Phelps' Model A. He peered between the leaves and saw Velma Phelps stop the Ford next to their house. She got out, a brown paper grocery bag in her arms, slammed the car door shut and entered her house by the back stoop.

Luthur crept into the first furrow for a better look. Velma left the back door standing open while she emptied the bag's contents onto the sink-board. Canned goods mostly, but she also had a loaf of store-bought lightbread. The alkaline taste of the baking-soda biscuit lingered in his mouth. What he wouldn't give for just one slice of lightbread. She picked up the loaf and disappeared from sight with it. Luthur groaned.

Sitting on the end of the drain-board in plain sight, though, was a large can of peaches. He could see the yellow halves on the label. Velma still wasn't in sight. Without giving himself time to think about it Luthur burst out of the cotton, sprinted to the back door and seized the can. Heart pounding, he raced for the cotton, arms cradling the precious cargo to his chest. He didn't stop running until he was deep into the field. On his knees he listened, panting, afraid he might be caught and punished. Silence.

His breathing eased and he examined his treasure. The green Del Monte label pictured yellow Elberta halves glistening in syrup. Mouth watering, he opened his pocketknife and drove the broken blade through the metal top. He sawed the knife until he could bend the lid back. The aroma, the heavenly smell of golden fruit, teased his senses. He raised the can for a long drink of liquid so sweet his eyes closed in ecstasy. Dirty fingers extracted first one peach half and then another. He crammed each succulent piece into his mouth, wolfing it down like a ravenous animal.

Sated at last, Luthur lay on his back in the furrow, pressed both hands against his swollen belly and moaned with contentment. The account settled, he said aloud, "I melieve nat was worth a nwarter."

That Woman

Imarried that woman eight weeks ago. Ed and Lila Phillips, who lived across the street, invited me to dinner every couple of weeks after Millie died. We had been frequent dinner guests in each other's home for twenty years, and I considered them friends. Then a year after Millie's death I walked over to their house and a second guest was there. Her.

It was plain as a wart on your nose that it was a contrived situation, but I played along. The ladies were smug and giggly through dinner. She was attractive enough and a practiced conversationalist. I've never been much of a talker. We were partners in the *Trivial Pursuit* game after dinner, and I let the three of them yak it up while I tried not to form a hasty opinion of her. I have to admit I found her to be pleasant company.

When I went home that night I made a bet with myself that she would call me. I didn't have to wait twenty-four hours to collect. "Hello, Walter," she effervesced. God she was bubbly, but I remembered how Millie always put on her telephone voice. "I just wanted to let you know I had a lovely evening yesterday. It was wonderful meeting you." *It was? Nobody else had ever been thrilled to meet a grouchy, monosyllabic old coot.* "I wonder if you could come to my apartment Friday evening? I'd love to cook dinner for you." *Look out.* Unless I was mistaken, that was a shot across the bow. The boarding party couldn't be far behind.

"Gosh, I'm sorry, but I'll be out of town for a few days." I didn't have one damned thing to do, but I'd spread a roadmap on the kitchen table and pick out a nice long-weekend destination just as soon as she got off the phone.

"Maybe some other time then, Walter." She sounded crushed, or rather she sounded like she wanted me to *think* she sounded crushed.

"You bet," I said in as chipper a voice as I could muster and then hung-up.

I could not hazard a guess how she learned my schedule. Five days to Biloxi and back, and the darned phone started ringing before I could set my luggage down. "Hi, Walter." Miss Congeniality. "Did I catch you at a bad time?" *How does she know? How the heck does she know?* "I have a spinach and pasta casserole in the oven, and I want you to come right over and share it with me. I won't take no for an answer, Walter." How can you refuse an offer like that? I considered the odds and bet myself that she'd have me in her bed before the evening ended.

Millie and I had been married almost forty years when she passed on. Millie was a marvelous cook. She had a talent for seasoning foods. Meatloaf in her hands became ambrosia for the gods. Savory and moist, the leftovers extended their goodness through several lunchtime sandwiches.

Spinach and pasta just didn't hack it with me. I mean it wasn't as bad as it sounded, but it was as bad as it looked, even by candlelight. The wine was a great help but caused me to come close to forfeiting my bet. We became intensely acquainted on her living room couch and almost didn't make it to the bedroom.

Once you've had sex with a woman, obligations begin to pile-up. It's like when *Coca-Cola* used to add cocaine to their product. One was never enough. You began to establish a pattern, and the pattern became habit.

"Walter, I know how shy you are. You've been wanting to ask me this, so let's not put it off any longer." *Oh, oh. Here comes trouble.* I'm like a blind dog in a meat-house about these things. I can sniff them out from a long way off. It's not knowing which way to run that makes me hesitate. "I've set a date for our wedding." It was only six weeks since I met her at Ed and Lila's.

I had moped around the house for a month after Millie's funeral. Dirty dishes accumulated. I kept the stereo tuned to an easy-listening station all day, trying to defeat the solitude. I'd prowl the house, staring at empty ghost-filled rooms. When spring arrived, digging in the garden, planting beds of flowers, pruning roses gently eased me back into an ordered existence. I got used to living alone. The prospect of marriage rated no more than 6.0 on my Richter scale.

The silken threads of convenient intimacy, wrapped enough times, form a near-unbreakable cocoon. The brain as well as the body is seduced. I couldn't say no.

"Really, Walter, all this must go." We'd returned from a week's honeymoon in Charlotte Amalie, St. Thomas. She stood in my living room, and with a grand gesture indicated Millie's and my furniture. Early American, it included a louvered stereo cabinet and a set of rock-maple tables. I stacked them in a spare bedroom. The next day a van delivered a load of chrome-and-glass concoctions, neo-something-or-other, décor that would do an upscale gynecologist's reception room proud.

I am a sports fan. I don't watch WWF Smackdown, but I enjoy boxing and I enjoy tobacco-chewing, down-in-the-dirt baseball. Had I been able to handle a Class AA fastball, I might have made it to the majors. "Really, Walter, isn't there something more uplifting on television tonight?" Sure enough, she found the movie, Sleeping With The Devil, on LIFE cable channel. What the heck, the Braves were getting hammered anyway.

I have a row of six Tropicana rose bushes across one end of my front yard. At dusk or on a dark day I've been known to stand for a considerable length of time admiring those plants. Low light seemed to make their blossoms glow. Don't ask me why, but those were soul-expanding moments for me. Where poetry, ballet and opera failed to inspire me, those roses succeeded.

"Walter, those roses are all the same color." I already knew that. "Don't you think a mixture of colors would be prettier?" I sure as hell did not.

"No," I said.

"Don't be difficult, Walter. Of course it would." It absolutely, positively would not.

"No," I repeated.

Thursday morning a Porterfield & Sons Landscaping truck pulled into my driveway. The driver, a middleweight who reminded me of Carl "Bobo" Olson, handed me a delivery form to sign.

1 – Gypsy Carnival
1 – Michaelangelo
1 – Fredric Mistral
1 – Brandy
1 – Pascali

1 – Sterling Silver

"I didn't order these." I handed the form unsigned back to Bobo. He turned and compared the number on my mailbox to the delivery address. I walked toward the house.

"Oh, wonderful. The roses are here." She emerged from the house and hurried past me toward the truck. I turned and followed.

"He said he didn't order them." Bobo handed her the form.

"Nonsense," she said with an edge to her voice. She signed the form. "Just replace those plants over there with these."

"No," I said.

"Don't be difficult, Walter." She turned to Bobo. "Go ahead and plant them."

"No," I repeated. Bobo was caught between a dilemma and an exigency. He darted fearful looks first at me and then at her, like a fighter who'd just taken a right cross.

"Plant them," she ordered.

Bobo took a step backward. "But..." he stammered. He clearly wanted no part of this deteriorating situation. He threw me a look of pleading desperation. I shook my head no. Bobo took refuge in the cab of his truck and made a lurching, gear-grinding departure.

She had both hands on her hips. "Walter, really, do you expect me to stay with you when you behave in this manner?" She peered at me intently, with more than a touch of hostility. "Well, do you?"

"No, Ma'am," I said.

A peaceful silence descended on the household. When the Cubs baseball game ended I spent the remainder of the afternoon dragging rock maple back into the living room and stacking gynecological furniture in the spare room.

Later I stood outside in the evening gloom admiring the Tropicanas. *The roses never looked more beautiful, Millie.*

Prunus Persica

"You need a whippin' for that! Now get on out in that back yard!" Pa removed his dirty sweat-stained hat and tossed it on a chair. Black sweat-plastered hair clung to his skull. A penumbral line across his forehead, like a partial eclipse, divided the paleness of his brow from the sunburned leather of his face. Obsidian eyes flashed on either side of his hooked nose. When Pa was angry, he struck fear into your very soul. Not always apparent, the violence in him lay close to the surface, a solar flare waiting to erupt.

Pa never carried a watch. He measured time by work accomplished, and the clock was always running. "We're a-burnin' daylight," he'd yell, urging me to work faster at whatever task he'd assigned. Or I might be trying to drive a bent staple into a fence post. He'd watch my inept efforts until he could stand it no longer. "Here!" He'd grab the hammer out of my hand and pound the staple himself. And he certainly had no tolerance for someone being unfocused on the job.

We share-cropped an Oklahoma farm during the Great Depression. Our family's standard of living, always near the subsistence level, diminished year by drought-plagued year. Prices for farm produce were low, crop-yield scant. Every additional penny in the family coffers might stave off disaster.

I'd been cultivating the cornfield that day, staring for unending hours at two mules' back-ends. You know how boring that is? Riding that two-row cultivator up and down the field? Nothing to do but hold the mules, Buck and Sally, in the furrows, smell their sweat, their farts.

First thing you know, the music would start playing — radio music I'd heard and stored away. It seemed to rise up out of that loamy earth, trumpets pealing, clarinets wailing — Clyde McCoy, Benny Goodman, Duke Ellington. My foot began tapping to Ring Dem Bells. You know how Ellington plays it, all jazzy but real nice. Next thing I knew, that darned Buck reached across a knee-high row of corn to grab a bite off a clump of Johnson grass.

Before I could get them back where they belonged, Buck had pulled Sally and the cultivator with him. I jerked them to a stop, swiveled on the metal seat and looked behind me, insides cringing at the devastation. Six or eight feet of two corn rows gouged open, plants laying with pale roots out of the ground, leaves crushed. Pa wouldn't miss that.

It was near quitting time, sun getting low. I finished the field, but the only music I heard was a kind of dirge, something that might be played on the way to a hanging.

When Pa came into the house just before supper, it didn't take him long to find his subject. "I seen what you done in the corn." His face darkened with pent-up anger. "I send you out there to do a man's work and all you do is lollygag around. We're dependin' on that corn for a livin'." And then he pronounced judgment, right in front of Ma and the girls.

Both my sisters were trembling, scared and wide-eyed. Ma bit her lip and went to the kitchen. She'd seen it all happen before. She didn't approve, but I knew she wouldn't challenge Pa.

I was fourteen then, that spring of 1935. I'd been whipped often enough but not in the last year or so, had come to believe I'd outgrown that stage. What dignity I had curdled like three-day-old milk. Ordered out in the back yard to be whipped like a dog. Self-esteem evaporated, and I felt like nothing, no better than the pages in that outhouse Sears Roebuck catalog.

Like most farmsteads, ours had a big back yard. No lawn, really, just patches of Bermuda growing in blue-white soil where wash water was thrown off the porch. On the backside of the yard stood a peach tree — prunus persica. That name always evoked visions in my mind of a delicate Persian princess biting into succulent fruit, juice running off her chin. Pa had another use for it.

He strode past me, angry rapid steps taking him to the peach tree. By the time he reached it he had his Case knife out of his pocket, blade open. He grabbed hold of a four-foot branch of this year's growth and slashed it off near its base. On the return trip he improved the aerodynamics of the instrument by stripping off its leaves.

It's funny when you're waiting in limbo for something bad to happen how time seems to drag in slow motion and your senses sharpen. This was that dusky, magic time of day. The sun had slid out of sight and left spreading colors behind, reaching hands of red and yellow raised in benediction. Cooling air made you forget the heat of noon. Fireflies danced along the weedy margins of the yard, their amatory acrobatics far too carefree for the impending event. I could count each long pointed leaf Pa tore from the branch, smell its pungent almond odor, smell my own fear.

He grabbed me by the wrist to hold me in range. A hornet's sting penetrated my shirt, extending across my back. Pa always wanted the object of his punishment to yell. I didn't even try to hold it in. I pranced counter-clockwise, yowling and flinching while he turned with me, the harsh green switch cutting through soft air, abusing buttocks, legs, shoulders… my worthiness as a son.

He released my wrist, chest heaving from the exer-tion. I could lift my eyes no higher than my shoe tops, couldn't face that stony glare I knew was above me. "You got to be more careful out there, boy!" he commanded.

"I know, Pa. I'll try." A cry for forgiveness.

"Tryin' don't mean nothin' if you don't put your mind to it!" He tossed the switch to one side and walked toward the house leaving me degraded, broken with no hope. I dropped to my knees sobbing, the lash's sting replaced by the ultimate pain of absolution denied.

Pa's old now — hair all white, that curved nose jut-ting out between sunken dark eyes. He's mellowed a lot over the years. I see him wince when I swat one of his grandchildren on the backside. He lives with me now. Depends on me. I know it's not easy for him, self-suffi-cient as he's always been. Time weighs heavy for him. He tries to keep busy, putters around, makes unneeded repairs. I've never said it to him, he's never said it to me, but there's a love between us. We laugh at the same jokes. We like listening to baseball games together.

The harsh image I had of him as a boy softened and diminished through the years. I came to realize he was a product of his time without the moderating effect of a formal education that he made possible for me to acquire. His methods of discipline were pretty much the community standard in his day and time.

But the past doesn't seem to matter much now. Well… maybe it does some, but I keep telling myself it doesn't. If we could not voice words of mutual forgiveness, I at least had found unspoken clemency for him.

I brought home a little paper bag of freestone peaches from the grocery store and offered him one. He bit into it and said, juice dribbling, "Remember them good Elbertas we growed at home? Finest peaches I ever et."

Yeah, Pa. I remember.

Oh Bury Me Not

I drove up to Farkleville as soon as I got the call from Francie. She's my only sister, two years younger than me. She told me Waldo, that's her husband, had passed on. I asked what happened to Waldo, and Francie said, "He fell out of a tree." I was not surprised to learn later that Waldo at the time was CUI, climbing under the influence. Francie wanted me to help her get through her time of sorrow. I did what any self-respecting brother would do, I said, "I'll be there just as soon as I can."

I arrived that evening. Farkleville is not real big, but it's quaint. The one main street runs up through a narrow canyon. Houses and businesses along the sides are all higher than the road, most of them with stilts under the front end. Most had open carports under the house.

Francie told me that we needed to make arrangements with the funeral home the next day. She seemed relieved to have somebody to share her burdens.

Next morning we went to the undertaker's. His place of business, Fosdick's Funeral Home, had uphill parking in front. The lower half of the building would have been a basement if it wasn't exposed to the weather on three sides. We entered a door marked OFFICE, PLEASE COME IN.

Inside, a speaker system carried the lively notes of a piano accompanied by a banjo and brass band playing Maple Leaf Rag. A desk and chairs occupied the middle of the room. A Fosdick Funeral Home calendar hung on the wall, featuring an overly abundant blonde lady, a real eye catcher uncovered the way she was.

Nobody was in sight. We looked at each other and took seats. Time passed. After Maple Leaf Rag came Tiger Rag, then The Entertainer followed by Tremonisha. I always did like Scott Joplin.

Francie looked at her watch and shrugged. I was content to study the calendar. The piano began playing Solace, then a door in the rear opened, and this tennis-player looking guy walked in. All smiles, he moved briskly.

"Good morning, good morning," he said. He wore Bermuda shorts, a tee shirt that read across the front YOU ONLY GO AROUND ONCE and white Reeboks. "My name is Gordon Fosdick," he said by way of introduction. He shook hands with us while he told us, "You can call me Foz." He asked, still flashing the million-dollar smile, "What can I do for you good people this morning?"

Francie and I exchanged glances, and she said in a weepy voice, "My husband died."

"Of course, of course," Foz enthused. "I knew it had to be something like that. Here," he said, and pulled out a desk drawer, reached in and came out with papers. "This will give you an idea of our available services and prices." He handed us each a paper. Out of the speakers came Steptime Rag.

We examined the listings while Foz smiled, hummed along with the music and kept the beat with his fingers on the desktop. Francie settled on the budget package, the particleboard coffin with mahogany finish, the ten-minute chapel service and roundtrip transportation of the family to the cemetery.

We concluded the arrangements to the tune of Palm Leaf Rag and rose to depart. Foz shook our hands and said, "Thank you so much, and have a nice day." Francie commenced crying. Overwhelmed with sorrow, I supposed.

The funeral service was lovely. The music piped into the chapel was more hushed than in Foz' office. It sounded like Xavier Cugat's Bim Bam Bum, best I could tell. Waldo looked very natural except for the absence of a shot glass in his hand.

After the service we waited for the coffin to be loaded into a borrowed florist's delivery van. Foz wore a dark suit for the occasion, although he still had on the Reeboks. He held the door while we got in the back seat of the family car, a BMW convertible. "It's such a beautiful morning," he said, "Why don't we just put the top down?"

"Fine," I said. It really was a nice day.

We followed the hearse with the pink and yellow daisies painted on its sides. Hunched over the wheel Foz said, "This car could hit sixty by the end of the block." Francie, still weeping from the funeral service, took hold of her hat. I think the only thing holding Foz back was the flower truck hogging the road in front of us.

When we got to the cemetery there was trouble. The backhoe operator broke a water line at just about the six-foot level. The grave filled halfway up with water before the leak could be stopped.

Foz seemed stymied at first. "We can't put the casket

in that water," he said. "The particleboard will melt like sugar." Always resourceful, he told us, "You folks just wait right here a few minutes, visit among yourselves and I'll be right back." He hopped into the BMW and accelerated down to the gate and out onto the highway.

Ten minutes later he was back with a roll of clear plastic that he spread on the ground. "You men bear a hand here," he directed, and together we set Waldo's container in the middle of the plastic. Foz folded the sides and ends around the casket and sealed it all with duct tape. "There," he said proudly, "That ought to last until the resurrection. Let's lower it in, boys."

Six of us slid the casket over and into the hole. Muddy water splashed over shoes and trouser legs of those nearest. Waldo, in his polyethylene cocoon, floated only half-submerged, like a breaching humpback whale. Francie broke down in racking sobs. I never had any idea she had that depth of feeling for Waldo.

Foz instructed the backhoe operator to hold the casket down with the bucket while two men shoveled in enough dirt to keep everything stabilized.

So now Waldo is duct-taped for eternity. Francie hasn't settled down yet, but in time I'm sure she'll stop crying over her loss.

The Bus Stops Here

"I think I'm in love with her, Harv."

"Uh-huh. Listen here, James Earl, women are like city buses; you miss one and there'll be another one along in ten minutes. Just enjoy the moment and forget about her." He held up two fingers to the bartender.

As soon as he had the cold bottle in his hand James Earl resumed arguing his case. "You don't understand, Harv, Darlene is special. I never ever ran across any woman like her."

Harv gave a long-suffering sigh. "Yeah, what's so special about her? She have three of something?"

"She's as normal as you or me," James Earl responded. He took a thoughtful sip from the bottle. "My grandpa used to talk about an old Lucky Strike radio commercial; so round, so firm, so fully packed." He took another meditative sip. "If Darlene ain't fully packed, I don't know the meaning of the term."

"You trying to tell me she's chunky?"

"No, no," James Earl replied, "not chunky, not chunky at all; just solid, solid as a country woman's butter."

In an abrupt change of direction Harv said, "Let me ask you this, James Earl, when was the last time we went camping up on the lake? A year? Two years? You know that creek that feeds in on the far side? There's more trout around there than you can count. What say we take off in the morning and spend a few days up there? Maybe the whole week."

James Earl straightened upright on his stool, looked at his friend, nodded in agreement; big smile, eyes bright. Then his face fell. "I can't do it, Harv."

"Why on earth not? The world ain't going to fall apart if you go fishing for a week."

"Well, Mr. Ferguson gave me the job at the feed store, and I can't let him down, take off for a week without notice." He glanced at his watch. "I've got to run Harv. Me and Darlene are going to a movie tonight. See ya."

Harv shook his head in disgust and waggled a finger at the bartender.

❋   ❋   ❋

James Earl couldn't have told anyone much about the movie afterward. He'd spent a stimulating two hours trying to out-maneuver Darlene. She'd devoted most of the time to attempted control of James Earl's inquisitive hands while she enjoyed more intense activity, only with romantic dialog, on the big screen.

They settled into a booth at Shorty's Café for post-movie coffee and a piece of pie. "Harv wants me to go fishing with him all next week," he said glumly, "but I can't go."

"The trip sounds great, James Earl. Why can't you go?"

He forked a savory chunk of apple pie to his mouth,

chewed and swallowed. "Well, I just can't take off like that and leave Mr. Ferguson holding the bag. He's been real good to me, and he depends on me."

Darlene frowned. "You can't get anyone to fill-in for you?"

"I don't know who it'd be." James Earl sipped his coffee. "I just don't know anybody who could handle the job."

"Wait a minute," Darlene said, rising excitement in her voice. "Just a cotton-picking minute." She smiled at him, eyes sparkling. "How about me? I can do it. I know I can."

James Earl stared at her, mouth open, a chunk of cinnamon-flecked apple exposed. He swallowed then began shaking his head. "No, Darlene, this is man's work. I wouldn't want you to get hurt on the job." He swallowed hard again to prevent himself from adding, "...or be embarrassed."

"I can do it, James Earl. Look at me." He looked. He looked some more. "I'm not one of those wispy little faint-hearted women who scream at the sight of a mouse. Look at me, James Earl. I am a WOMAN." She sure enough was that.

❄   ❄   ❄

Mid-afternoon three days later the two campers idly cast their spinning rods from a sitting position on the sun-warmed lakeshore. "This is the life, ain't it, James Earl?"

"You bet. We haven't had a strike in three days, and the deer flies are eating me alive. What else you got in that tackle box, Harv?"

"We've tried everything, unless you want to go second-time-around."

James Earl reeled his lure in and laid the rod on the ground beside him. "You know, I'm worried about Darlene. I'm afraid she's either working herself to death, or else Mr. Ferguson has fired her. I'd hate to see that happen." He looked over at Harv. "You had about enough of this? I mean without any fish to eat we're running low on grub. What say we head back in the morning?"

Harv reeled his line in. "Well, if it'll stop your grieving and whining, I guess I'm ready."

❄ ❄ ❄

The parking lot at Ferguson's Feed Store had a Wal-Mart look to it. Pickups waiting to pull in, loaded pickups waiting to leave. Mr. Ferguson said, "Danged if I knew there were this many horse and dog and cow owners in the county." He watched as Darlene, followed by three leering, red-necked farm boys, pushed a hand-truck loaded with sacks of feed. If those boys grinned any wider they'd all need surgery, he thought.

Business had picked up noticeably the first day she was on the job, busy as a one-legged man in a football game. Darlene caught many a glance as she hustled about in her fully packed jeans and tee shirt. The next day produced the most sales of any day this year. Today would be even better. The smell of money wafted in the air. He'd call his suppliers to refresh and enlarge his inventory.

He'd been afraid she wouldn't be able to handle the heavy work, but it was mostly "can I carry that for you, miss?" or "let me give you a hand with that, ma'am." Darlene was a bonanza, a sure enough mother lode.

Loose Ends

James Earl parked out along the highway and walked to the feed store. What the Sam Hill was going on here? Was Mr. Ferguson having a half-price sale? Had there been a major accident? He went up the loading-dock steps and saw Mr. Ferguson immediately. He leaned against the office door, smiling like he'd just been named citizen of the year. "Mornin', James Earl," he said. "What're you doing back so early?"

"Well, I just thought you might be needing me."

Mr. Ferguson shoved his hands in his pockets, rolled a toothpick around in his mouth and laughed. "See that girl in there, that Darlene? Well, I owe you a bonus for sending her to me. I've offered her a permanent job here plus a commission, and I've decided you'd make her a good assistant, same pay you're getting now. What do you think about that, James Earl?"

❆   ❆   ❆

"She took my job, Harv. Mr. Ferguson gave her MY job plus a commission, and he wants me to be her assistant."

Harv swiveled on his stool and waved four fingers at the bartender. He placed a cold one in James Earl's hand as soon as they were delivered. "That's the way it goes, James Earl," he commiserated. "I'm telling you it's a dog-eat-dog world out there."

A near sob in his voice, James Earl said, "I gotta hand it to you, Harv. You were right about women. But you said there'd be another one come by in about ten minutes. Didn't you say that, Harv?"

Harv took a pull on his bottle. "Yeah, but sometimes it takes a little longer."

The Ceremony

Me and Pritch were at Bogarde's Roadhouse Café on an early Saturday afternoon. We'd both of us just finished a big bowl of crab gumbo and were relaxing with amber bottles, each beaded with moisture.

Between sips Pritch opined that this was the year the Braves would make a comeback. I had just told him the Braves would be eating the Cardinals' dust when a pearl gray Lexus pulled up and parked beside the front door. I didn't know at the time it was a Lexus — all these new cars look the same to me.

In walked this vaguely familiar fella, only he's all duded out in expensive western clothes — hat, boots, suede jacket, shirt with piping, the works and none of it familiar. I mean I don't know anybody who dresses like that.

"Afternoon," he said. Pritch and me both nodded. "Irvin Danforth," he said, sticking out his hand. Pritch turned away and swatted at a circling fly while I shook the man's hand. Pritch he can be an embarrassment social-wise at times. "You're Chauncy Bellew," Irvin declared.

He had me there, so I said, "That's right." I remembered Irvin. He was that skinny little twerp in high school who always had his work done on time and always got good grades. "Howdy, Irvin," I greeted. "What are you doing back in this neck of the woods?"

Irvin had a presence about him now. Back in high school he always seemed nervous as a spinster in an obstetrician's waiting room. Now he acted like he was the boss, he knew he was the boss and he liked being the boss.

Irvin, cool as a cucumber, said, "I'm trying to find Betty Funston. Do you know if she's still around?" Pritch almost choked on his beer, coughed a couple of times and grabbed a handful of paper napkins to clean up after himself. Pritch he really needs to work on his self-control.

"I believe she is," I answered, "if she's the one I'm thinking about."

Irvin's eyes showed excitement now. "Cute little girl," he said, "maybe five-two, athletic, big brown eyes, dynamite figure."

Pritch he's trying to control a laughing jag that sounded like a cat being strangled. The Betty Funston we knew was short and had doubled her weight since high school. She was known to her intimates as Sweaty Betty. And she had a goodly number of intimates. "Well, she still has big brown eyes," I told Irvin.

Irvin seemed to be letting his excitement take control. No longer the cool businessman, he acted more like a teenager about to ask for his first date. "I'm going to marry her," he announced. "I brought a ring with me, and if she'll have me I'm going to marry her." He edged closer to confide, "See, my wife and I divorced recently, and ever since I just can't get Betty out of my mind. Betty and I had some great times back in high school." Excited. The man was excited. "Can you tell me where she lives?" he inquired.

I turned and looked at the clock on the wall. "She usually stops by here about this time of day," I said. "Likes to have a bit of refreshment before going to work." I didn't tell him she worked nightshift at the sawmill and never reported for work with less than four beers in her. She used to drink six or more until the accident. About two months ago she lost the thumb and index finger on her left hand without being aware of it until she almost bled out. Now she was more moderate in her drinking so as to stay alert on the job.

"I guess I'll just wait here for her then," Irvin said before ordering a whiskey sour from the bartender. Pritch he could barely contain himself waiting for the showdown. I swear that boy has never outgrown his juvenility.

Around three o'clock a dusty two-seater pickup pulled up. The doors opened and out poured four men and Sweaty Betty, all wearing hardhats, jeans and work-shirts. They came inside loud and boisterous, ordering beers all around. Pritch jabbed me in the ribs and pointed with his thumb at Irvin. Irvin looked like a man beset by information overload.

Sweaty Betty looked us over, smiled and waved to me and Pritch. She held her eyes on Irvin though, studying him like he was a frog in biology class. "Hot damn," she hollered. "Is that you, Irvin?" She waddled over close to him, a beer bottle in hand. "It is. It is you." She threw her arms around him and hugged and squeezed until she'd spilled beer down the back of his $800 jacket.

Irvin turned white as a bed-sheet. In fact he'd paled

the minute that bunch had walked in the door. Pritch inquired, innocent as a lamb, "When's the wedding, Irvin?" Pritch he really needs to be more polite. He might benefit from instruction in the social graces.

"B-b-betty," Irvin stammered. "Is that really you?"

"All 212 pounds of me," she brayed while she hugged him tighter and sloshed more beer down his back. "Remember them good times we had in the back of your car, Irvin? Boy howdy, you were some kind of lover-boy." Irvin had acquired a look of panic surrounded by desperation with a touch of terror. His eyes rolled side-to-side, searching past Betty's bosom for an exit path, some means of escape.

Pritch he couldn't seem to let well enough alone. "Are you going to invite us to the wedding, Betty?"

"Wedding?" She seemed to recall hearing the word just seconds before. "Wedding?" she repeated. She loosened her grip on Irvin and stepped back, eyes wide, a look of bliss dawning on her kewpie-doll face. She stared right into Irvin's eyes. "You're asking me to marry you? Oh, yes. Oh, yes, Irvin. Yes, yes, yes." Irvin's eyes rolled back and he went to the floor in a heap.

Well, a glass of water in his face and the rest of his whiskey sour down the hatch partially revived him, although I've known people in intensive care with more color in their cheeks. We got him to his feet and sitting in a booth.

I noticed Pritch having intense conversation with Cooter Moss, one of the boys from the sawmill. Pritch returned to the table and said to Betty, "If you want to have the ceremony now there's a preacher right here." He nodded toward Cooter.

"Cooter is a preacher? I never knew that." She turned toward him. "Oh, Cooter, could you?" She turned back to Irvin. "Could we Irvin? Oh, please, please, please, Irvin." Irvin's head slumped down which Betty apparently read as a positive answer. "Let's do it now, this very minute," she shouted. Betty seemed full of joy, eager and anxious to begin her matrimonial journey.

Jiggs Davidson, part of the sawmill gang and a musician of some note, played "Here Comes The Bride" with one hand under his armpit.

We got Irvin in a standing position, Betty beside him. Cooter demonstrated no more knowledge of wedding vows than he had of the King James Bible, but he stumbled through. "Y'all put the ring on her finger," he instructed Irvin. When Betty presented her left hand Irvin seemed stunned at the sight of the appendage. Some might say it resembled a three-tined garden trowel. Irvin's mouth worked, he pointed at the hand but words failed to come. His eyes rolled back, and it was revival time again.

It took awhile, once Irvin was converted from horizontal to vertical, for him to find a finger the ring would fit. With help from bystanders he was able to get it to the first knuckle of her little finger. Everybody cheered, and everybody but Irvin kissed the bride.

We ushered them out to the Lexus, showering the couple with shredded napkins and the like. Betty insisted on driving. She slid under the wheel in a euphoric state. Irvin, in the passenger seat, looked like a man recovering from a two-week bout with the flu. He wore the thousand-yard stare of someone whose world had been turned upside down.

They sped away to Lord knows where. Pritch said

in a bemused voice, "That was nice. That was really nice." His voice saddened as he added, "I really hate to see her go. I mean we gained a space at the bar, but we lost Sweaty Betty."

The Piano

I sit in my new apartment, first night alone, just me and a cold Sam Adams. Indifferent and unfocused I stare at the television. Cheerless. The No Spin Zone fails to revive me.

Like tinkling raindrops music seeps through the wall, awakes my conscious mind. Someone's playing a piano in the next apartment. I mute the television and melt back into my recliner to listen. It can't be Fats Waller, but he's playing "All My Life", stride style. I picture dark stubby fingers in blurred flight, a flock of starlings rising. Memory recalls the lyrics in Waller's hoarse voice. I am transported. And then the music ends, folds in on itself, fades into wistful silence.

I take another beer from the refrigerator, hurry into the hallway and knock on his door — too loudly, I think. The sound of security locks opening, and she's standing in front of me. Brown eyes with flecks of gold calmly appraise. Behind her a Baldwin upright stands in ebony stillness.

"You're the pianist?" I ask, surprised in my gender-biased assumption. She's almost as tall as I, blonde hair tumbling onto the shoulders of her Cal Poly sweatshirt. Her fingers are not dark, not stubby.

"That's who I am," she answers, a quirky smile turning up one corner of her full mouth. "Was I disturbing you?" There doesn't seem to be a lot of regret in the question.

"No… I mean, yes." I always was good with words. "What disturbed me was the music stopped. You know, like that old tune "The Song Has Ended But The Melody Lingers On."

She opens the door wider and says, breathes actually, "I think you had better come in."

I step inside, uncap the Sam Adams and she accepts, takes a sip. "Could you play some more?"

She motions toward a couch and I sit. She glides easily onto the piano bench. After a few tentative notes she begins "What A Little Moonlight Can Do" in Teddy Wilson fashion. Improvisational runs above the left-hand notes excite, captivate, enthrall. The second time through, she sings the words. Her voice is sultry, somewhere this side of Billie Holiday. I close my eyes and let the magic wash over me.

When it ends we remain silent and motionless for long seconds. She rises and takes two diamond rings from the piano top and slips them on her finger. "I think you'd better leave now. My husband will be home soon." She hands me her near-full bottle and escorts me to the door.

"Thank you, it was beautiful," I tell her before returning to my apartment. I survey the emptiness then I sigh and sink into my recliner. It's just me, Sam Adams and Bill O'Reilly.

Uncle Dob

Mama's brother, Uncle Dob, moved in with us awhile back. That was right after Aunt Maisy left him. She took up with a guitar-playing singer who had a weeklong engagement at the Pedal-To-The-Metal Club out on Route 31. She'd kicked over the traces a few times before, and Uncle Dob didn't seem too broke-up about her leaving.

Mama told Daddy, "Poor Dob, he's rattlin' around that trailer by hisself, nobody to look after him, and we got this spare bedroom gatherin' dust. I'm goin' to ask him to move in with us."

Daddy, he didn't say anything. You could tell it wasn't the high point of his day, but he never was one to go against Mamma much. He just nodded a few times, but when he went out the door he was mumbling "old windbag" or some such.

So Uncle Dob moved into the spare bedroom. He didn't own much in the way of worldly goods. Besides his clothes, he had a set of mechanic's tools, a museum-piece International pickup and a long-standing drinking habit. Uncle Dob had a fondness for beer, and when you walked into the spare bedroom, what you saw was the end of his toolbox and a case or two of Old Milwaukee sticking out from under his bed.

Uncle Dob was between jobs when he moved in. He was a good mechanic and never had any trouble getting work with one of the local auto-repair shops. They all knew he'd show up every day for maybe a month, but that was about his limit. One day, usually a Monday after payday, he'd come up missing, and they'd just get along without him for a week or two until he showed up again.

He was younger than Mama by four years, but he looked older, and Mama didn't have those purple lines on her nose.

There'd always been talk around town that Uncle Dob had been awarded the Bronze Star medal for bravery in Viet Nam. Nobody in the family had ever seen the medal or so much as a newspaper article about it, and Uncle Dob wouldn't talk about it. But he was given a certain amount of hero status by most of our family.

We were a little surprised when a woman reporter from the local paper phoned. Wanted to know if she could do an interview with Dob for the Veterans Day edition. Even more surprising, Uncle Dob said, "Sure, why not," and agreed to see her the next evening after work.

Well don't you know that Uncle Dob came home soused the next day. The reporter was waiting for him, tape recorder plugged in and ready. Uncle Dob flopped into an overstuffed chair in the living room, and the reporter pulled up a straight-back chair directly in front of him. She immediately waved her hand back and forth in front of her face and slid her chair out of range of Uncle Dob's breath.

She held the microphone close in front of her, stated the time and date and identified herself and the interviewee. "Could you tell me," she began, "about the events leading up to you being awarded the Bronze Star?" She leaned toward him, but tentatively, reaching the microphone in his direction.

'Yes, ma'am," he said. "Me and another Pfc name of Gideon Jenks was on night patrol with our squad. Gideon he was from up around Wentzville, Missouri. I knew a family up in that country, Rayfield was their name. No relation to the Rayfields that live hereabouts. Morgan Rayfield, the one from the Wentzville Rayfields, not the local bunch, was mean as a snake. Get a little booze in him and he might set fire to your outhouse, let the air out of your tires, or no telling what. He'd been known to steal watermelons. Now the Rayfields hereabout are just opposite, not a mean bone among the bunch of them.

"Well sir," Uncle Dob had his eyes closed, leaning back in his chair while he talked. The reporter sat poised in front of him, microphone extended at arm's reach, mouth open. "Well sir, Harley Rayfield, he's the one used to work for the circus. His job was being shot out of a cannon. They miscalculated the trajectory one day and he overshot the net. Never was quite right after that. Anyway Harley married the daughter of the Calhoun County district attorney. Wesley Wickum I believe his name was. The daughter's name was Marvalene… no, wait a minute, maybe it was Mildred. Don't make no difference. Anyway Marvalene or Mildred, it don't matter, wore big hats, I remember. Shady they were. Had tattoos on her arms. She might have had some other places, but I only saw her arms. Dragons and snakes crawling up beyond her elbows. Other than that she was a right pretty woman. I knew a fella

216   *Loose Ends*

had a hula girl tattooed on his arm. He could make her wiggle by flexing his muscles.

"Marvalene, or was it Mildred, she had a sister. I believe her name was Geraldine. She's the one had the three-legged dog. Lost a hind leg to a lawnmower. The dog he seemed to get along fine except he had trouble scratching one side. Geraldine's husband, Tilfred Potts, he came into some money and took up flying for a hobby. Bought hisself a plane and announced he was going to fly it through the first tornado that come along. A couple of weeks later he got his wish and dived right in among tree limbs, roofing material and who knows what all. That was back in June, and he hasn't been seen since. Geraldine says she'll give him what for if he ever shows up again.

"Say, my throat's getting dry. Would you mind handing me a cold beer out of the refrigerator?"

The reporter pointed at herself. "Me?"

"Yes, you, honey. Just run on in the kitchen there and fetch me one."

She was back in a heartbeat, a frosty can extended toward him. She was still hoping to get her interview for Veterans Day, but she was too late. Uncle Dob, mouth open, was sawing logs.